Cats in the Belfry

My love and appreciation to my husband, Terrell, for giving me the life to be able to write a book that I hope will be enjoyed by others.

Chapter 1

As the white Chrysler cruised down the two-lane highway, the inside of the car was quiet as a mouse. Looking out at the sun, Frances debated out loud: "Do you think we can make it in two hours or do you think we need to stop at a motel again and start early in the morning?" Not waiting for an answer, she continued, "I really would like to sleep in my own bed tonight. I did not figure on spending so much time in Atlanta. But the attorney was so nice, and even though he did not have a lot of additional information, he was very courteous about my having you in the office with me while we talked. He understood the danger of being in an automobile in the hot sun." He did mention that the last two sets of heirs had never visited the property and only wanted to release themselves of the responsibility of mailing the money for the taxes each year.

Having read the paper with the description of the property countless times, she could quote it from memory: "Selling beautiful property to settle estate. Ten acres, secluded, lots of live oaks, large windows, beautiful wood floors. Open plan with multiple levels allowing versatile use of space. Great location for antiques. Will not sell in lots—all or nothing. All contents go with sale. Contact M. M. Whitehead, PO Box 149334, Atlanta, GA, 30303. Doesn't it sound wonderful?"

An hour later, Frances decided to continue traveling. She was enjoying the peace and quiet of the ride and the beautiful countryside. The scream from the backseat would have made a normal person's hair turn white. Goose bumps popped out on Frances's arms immediately, as she tried to remain in control of the car and bring it to a stop at the side of the highway. As she turned around to survey the occupants of the backseat, she was faced with three sets of eyes. There was no doubt what had happened. "Star, I have asked you time and again—do not do that! We almost had a wreck. There is no way he can invade your space. He has his carrier and you have yours. What did he do? Look at you? Why do you have to act like the injured party? Don't you know he was as afraid as I was? If you were smart, you'd realize I know your tricks. At least, Sunshine did not lose hair in the process this time. Now settle down—we're going to be in our new home soon. We'll have lots of room for everyone."

The rest of the trip was again silent. As the sign appeared: "Synaxis, Georgia, population 547," all three cats stood, stretched, and looked outside. Frances was curious as to what they were thinking. She tried to comfort them, saying, "See, we are here. Just a little while longer and you will be in your new home." As she came within sight of the intersection, she glanced at the directions again. *Turn left at traffic light.* The light was green, but just as she got to the light, it suddenly turned red and she had to slam on her brakes. All three cats lost their footings and registered their complaint about her driving. "Sorry, folks, but can't start out in our new home breaking the law." As she sat waiting for the light to change, she stared at the buildings. They all looked as if they had not had any maintenance in many years. There was no sign of light or life at any of the windows. The grocery store reminded her of the stores when she was a child in small towns. Before the era of supermarkets, she liked to watch the clerks pick up your items, place them by the register, and write down a figure on a tablet. She noticed a small hardware next to the grocery store. She glanced back at the red light before looking at the next store. "5 and 10 Cent Store" was all the sign showed. The last business before the end of the block was a drugstore. At her left was a service station with two antique-looking gas pumps.

Frances looked back at the traffic light, which was red, and at her watch. Had she missed the signal changing? Looking over her shoulder, she saw three heads lowered and three sets of eyes staring at the signal. She turned to join the trio in watching the signal.

She finally released her seat belt, opened her door, and stepped one foot out and stared at the light. *This is crazy*, she thought. She got back into her car, fastened the belt, and put the car back in gear. The light finally changed, and she turned left, then made another sharp left as the directions for the attorney had said. Everyone said she was crazy for buying a house without seeing it first. Her answer was that it sounded just like what she had dreamed of owning. She wished the attorney had been able to furnish pictures, but after looking at the survey and the outline of the buildings on the property, she was convinced this was right.

Looking at the odometer, she calculated two miles and prepared to watch for a road turning left. Suddenly, she realized that the road she was on was not paved. Although it was not rough, she could see the plume of dust from the back of her car. As she neared the end of the two miles, she slowed the car even more and watched for the road. *There, that small opening in the trees must be it.* Suddenly, a narrow road appeared, and she turned the car slowly onto single-lane road—or perhaps trail would be a better word. "I am to go two-tenths of a mile," she repeated to herself. No comment from the backseat. She looked in the mirror and saw three anxious faces looking from side to side. There were patches of water on both sides of the road. Cypress trees stood like silent watchmen with little light showing through the vegetation.

You would think it was the middle of the night. The car finally came into an area with less vegetation and what appeared to be small fields on both sides, allowing a little more light.

She started back into a wooded area, but on higher ground. There she saw an old church surrounded by live oaks with long clumps of moss hanging from the limbs. As she rolled past the church, she admired the beautiful windows and all the trees. The lane became even narrower and branches from small bushes were beginning to scrape the sides of the car. Among the azalea bushes, she could see tombstones. "Weird! I hope there's another route into my property so you don't have to travel this way home every time.

There was total silence in the backseat. Not a sound of movement could be heard. But she could feel the eyes staring at the back of her head. The narrow lane wandered among the graves, and finally, she saw a little daylight remaining at an opening in the trees. As she came back out, she was excited and hoped she was about the see her new home. But all she saw was the church again.

Looking at the directions again, she went through them step by step. There was nothing else. She pulled up to the side of the church and got out of the car. Hearing a low growl from the backseat, she could feel chills going up her back, to the top of her head. "Don't do that! I'll figure out something."

She caught herself walking on tiptoes as she went to the front of the building. Easing up the steps, she stood staring at the massive door. Making a turn in place, she took in all the surroundings. "No, it couldn't be. The attorney never said it was a *church*. But then he never said it was a *house* either." Standing there in the silence, she finally reached into her pocket and felt the large key he had given her. Pulling the key out of her pocket, she stared at the ornate beauty of the old key. She had thought it was a beautiful key for her beautiful new home. Slowly, she raised the key and slid it into the opening. Taking a breath, she turned the key and felt the door give way from the boundaries of the lock. "What a nice mess this has turned out to be."

Before going inside, she returned to the car and pulled as close as possible to the front steps. Opening the back door of the car, she took each carrier to the top of the steps. Then she got their food, litter pans, water, and her overnight bag. From the accumulation, she picked up the carrier containing Star and said, "Ladies first." Stepping inside, she reached for a light switch and pushed it. Nothing happened! The attorney said the electricity had been turned on. After flipping the switch again and again, it finally made connection. Star summed up her feelings by letting loose with a low growl. They stared at years' accumulation of boxes, old pieces of furniture, and who knows what else piled into the large room. There was barely room to walk. Moving to the first flat surface, she placed Star's carrier down so she could retrieve the rest of her little family. As she turned to go to the door, Star let out a piteous small cry of fear. Frances soothed her by saying she would be right back.

After she had retrieved the cats, placing each on a high surface for them to see, she brought all the other belongings inside. Then she set out to find where she could sleep for the night before going to a telephone in the morning to call the attorney and tell him she had changed her mind. Wandering through the maze of boxes and furniture, she finally found a door at the other end of the sanctuary. As she grasped the doorknob and prepared to turn, Star let out one of her operatic cries that sent chills up her back again. She threw open the door with such a bang, it hit the wall behind and slammed shut again. Getting her breath, she opened the door again and reached inside for a switch. This time, a long hall lit up with small lights appearing just often enough to keep you from killing yourself as you made your way through the labyrinth of the same type of clutter that was in the sanctuary.

Standing on her tiptoes, she could see closed doors along the hall. Some of them could not be reached because of the clutter in front of them. Those she could reach, she opened and peered inside, only to discover the same view as before. She was careful to close each door, knowing if one of the cats were to accidentally get out of their carrier, she would never find them. Finally, at the end of the hall, a door opened to what appeared to have been a kitchen, probably where social functions were held. Thank goodness, there was less clutter here. There were numerous tables and straight-backed chairs, a sink on the wall (no cabinet beneath), a small refrigerator—from the era of rounded corners, perhaps early fifties—and a stove, same vintage. She could hear the hum of the refrigerator, so at least she might have cold water tonight. Hurrying to the sink, she turned on the faucets and a gust of air and water sputtered. After a few minutes, the stream of water became steady. Putting her fingers under the stream, she was pleased to find she also had hot water. Good, she could get the day's travel grime off her body.

The transfer of carriers and all the trappings consumed more time than she would have liked. After she finished the transfer, she made her way back through the sanctuary turning out the lights and locking the front door. She was surprised that it was completely dark. Getting into the car, she drove around the church to a door into the kitchen at the back of the church. As she opened the car door, she could hear all three cats in unison. Getting the first load, she made her way up the steps into the kitchen. The sound immediately stopped and the faces stared back. "You knew I would not leave you. Why did you have to make such a racket? Lucky for us we don't have close neighbors or they would call the police. Just be patient. When I unload what we need for tonight, I will let you out so you can eat and whatever.

After she unloaded the blankets, sheets, pillows, coffeepot, radio, and groceries, she locked the two doors and placed chairs beneath the door handles. She washed the sink and the table next to it. Faithful to her promise, she opened three carriers and three cautious cats slowly stepped out onto the table. Each cat walked slowly around the top of the table and looked up and down, side to side. They would crouch down and look as far underneath the table as possible. Sunshine, at one point, walked up behind Zeus and sniffed his back. Zeus immediately did a 90-degree midair turn and the chase was on. All around the room, they jumped from object to object until finally they ended beside Star who was slowly nibbling at the food.

Placing the cooler with her food on the table, she looked inside and decided the cats ate better than she did. She prepared a sandwich and sat staring around the room. She saw two other doors in addition to the one going to the hall and the back of the church. She wished she had investigated before letting the cats out of their carriers. She had checked the locks on each window in the kitchen, then looked around for something to cover the windows. What if there were windows that were not locked in one of the other rooms? Someone could come in and rob or harm them. Rob them, what a joke. She barely had enough money to keep body and soul together until she could get her money back on this property.

As soon as she finished eating, she put the food in the refrigerator and looked around at the doors. Crossing to the first door, she looked to see where the cats were located. They were sitting in a circle around a small chest, peering beneath, their chins almost touching the floor. Slowly opening the door, she peered inside. Turning on the switch, she found this was a small pantry. A similar collection of junk filled this room as well. She stood on her toes and visually checked the lock on the window; it appeared to be locked. By the time anyone made their way across the boxes, she would hear them, anyway. Looking back to make sure the cats were still stalking their prey, she closed the door, again placing a chair beneath the handle.

Opening the second door, she discovered a small bath. This room was not as filled as the others. Evidently, the kitchen and bath were used when additional junk was brought to the church for storage. She checked the window, then went back to her stack of bedding, and selected a sheet to drape over two nails at the top of the window. At least, she had one room with privacy. She felt the smooth caress of a cat rubbing past her leg. Star made one final swipe and made her way around the small room to investigate. She was replaced by Zeus who made a brief swipe before following. Sunshine was right behind. One cat jumped into the huge bathtub, and soon, all three were playing catch.

Frances walked around the kitchen, opening some of the drawers, which were full of items. She lifted the lids to some of the boxes and found they were also full. It would have taken years to accumulate all this junk. Who would want to bring it to an isolated church and store it for years? The attorney said the last two heirs had not bothered to come to check the property. In one box, she found a lamp, which she removed and plugged into an electric outlet on the wall. On a shelf, she saw some lightbulbs; she placed one in the lamp and turned it on. This would be much better than the overhead light when she went to bed. There was no way she would stay here without a light. Peering around some of the boxes, she found an antique chair. "This looks more comfortable than the kitchen chairs," she said to herself. When she started dragging boxes to make way for the chair, she immediately had three cats trying to get into the chair and investigate. "This is for me! Get your own!"

She went through the small bag and found her last outfit. Taking the towel and washcloth she had brought from the car, she sat out to wash. Naturally, the three cats took positions around the room and washed themselves. Going back into the kitchen, she arranged several blankets on one of the tables and placed her pillow on one end of the blankets. A sheet would be plenty of cover.

Sitting down in the comfortable chair, she propped her feet on a box and lay her head back to think of her predicament—and plan what she would say to Mr. Whitehead the next day. Surely, he would understand she could not live in a church, especially a church filled with years of junk. She opened her eyes and saw the three cats sitting patiently on a table close by. "My babies have had a rough three days. As a matter of fact, the last six months have not been so great. If I hadn't had you, I wouldn't have made it. I will always love you and take care of you." Each cat stood and turned in a small circle, emitting a low meow.

After a few minutes, Frances climbed onto the table and carefully lowered herself down onto the blankets. Pulling the sheet up around her, she lay back with a sigh. *Who would have thought this time last year, I would be broke, with no home and not a friend around* (meow). "You three are family," she told them.

Every sound from the outside was magnified. She could hear the wind in the trees. There were bushes brushing the outside of the building—at least, she hoped they were bushes. A window gave a slight rattle and shadows danced on the walls and ceilings. "I'm not afraid. Really, I'm not." Star stepped on top of her legs and settled down. Zeus curled up at one side, Sunshine on the other.

Chapter 2

The sound of one cat crunching food and one scratching in the litter pan woke Frances. She opened her eyes and wondered how the sunlight had not waked her. She turned her head and looked out one window; the sun was peeking through the leaves. Cardinals were flying around in the trees and several other birds were singing. Star was perched on the window ledge in a deep trance. She looked at Frances with green eyes and gave one of her silent chatters that told Frances she wanted to go outside. "You know that is not possible. You do not have a deck to protect you. A wild animal could catch you outside. We'll be leaving soon, and I will find us a home where you can go outside and enjoy nature.

Sipping coffee and eating the last piece of bread with peanut butter, Frances contemplated how she should handle the day. Looking at her outfit, crumpled from sleep, she decided she should pull a suitcase out of the trunk and dress better to go into town to call the attorney. While she was there, she would pick up a few groceries to last them until she could get back to Atlanta to get her money. She was glad she had a big supply for the cats. Sneaking out the back door, she immediately heard three cries of abandonment. She could hear the claws of one cat scratching the door. She gave them a soft encouragement and told them she would be right back.

While opening the trunk and getting more clothes, Frances had and uneasy feeling that she was being watched. She looked at the windows to see if the cats had climbed up to be able to see her. There was not a face to be seen. Then she heard all three at the back door. Almost running back inside, she held down her hand to stop any of the cats from escaping.

After quickly brushing her teeth and pulling her dress over her head, she explained, "I think it would be best if you remained here while I go into town. I won't be long. We can lock the back door so you'll be safe. When I get back, we will pack and go back to Atlanta."

None of the cats would look at her. She knew they did not like the plan. She went out the back door, tried the key in the lock, only to find it did not fit. Easing back inside, she turned the lock and put a chair in front of the door. She removed the chair from the door going into to the hall and opened the door just enough to get out of the room without the cats escaping. Again, she heard cries and claws. Winding her way to the front of the church, she unlocked the door and went outside. After relocking the door, she realized she would have to walk around the building to get her car. Weeds were as high as her waist, and they would probably be higher if it were not for the dense leaves of the trees hindering undergrowth.

Carefully placing her feet where she was watching, she wondered if there were snakes in the underbrush. She could see rose bushes strangled by the weeds in the church yard. Several tall azaleas were growing randomly. She passed through an opening of hedge that was almost as high as the church. Inside was what must have been a small meditation garden at one time. She could see a birdbath and a bench. The weeds did not seem to be as dense at this point. Going through another opening in the hedges, she could see the end of the building. Rounding the corner, she walked over to her car and opened the door. The cats, sensing that she was now at this door, were crying and scratching.

As she got to the main intersection going into town, Frances decided she would check at the grocery store for a public telephone. The traffic light was green, and she pulled up in front of the store. At a glance, one would think they were not open. She got out, went to the door, and opened it to step inside. Gloom hung over the place like a fog. She stood in place and looked around. Finally, a voice said, "Kin I he'p ye?" Frances jumped and looked at the counter. Sitting at the end in an old rocking chair was a little old lady, no bigger than a good-sized child.

Frances moved toward the lady and asked, "Where could I find a public telephone?

The old lady squinted and said, "A what?"

"A telephone" Frances stammered. "I need to call Atlanta."

The old woman said, "Ain't got no public telephone. Doctor over to the drugstore's got one. Nobody ain't got no call to use it. If'n we got sump'n to say, we just look ya up."

Frances looked around again to see if there was anything she could buy to eat. Nothing looked all that appealing. She turned to the old lady and said, "Well, I'll go up there to check and then I can come back here to buy my groceries. Be right back." Turning, she opened the door and stepped outside. As she walked up the sidewalk, she glanced at the stores and could not see any sign of activity.

Upon entering the drugstore, she felt the atmosphere was somewhat brighter. A man's voice called out from the back, "Yes."

Frances walked down the aisle and saw a white-haired man in a white jacket standing behind a counter. "I'm looking for a public telephone. I need to call Atlanta.

"We don't have a public telephone, but I could let you use mine," he replied softly.

"I'll be glad to pay for the call," Frances offered.

"Do you have the number?" he asked.

"Yes," she said, as she reached into her purse and pulled out the letter with the attorney's name and telephone number at the top.

Frances noticed the man let his eyes wander over the contents of the letter as he was turning the crank on the telephone mounted on the wall. "Mary, this is Doc in Synaxis. Somebody needs to talk to an attorney in Atlanta." Looking at Frances, he said, "Mary's making the call for you."

Frances knew that before she could get back to the church and load the cats all 547 people in Synaxis would know where she came from, who she talked to, and what she wanted. They were also going to be laughing that she did not bother to find out whether she was buying a house or a church.

Holding out the receiver, he motioned for Frances to come behind the counter to the wall to talk on the telephone. Frances took the receiver and stood on her tiptoes to get her mouth high enough to talk. She heard Mr. Whitehead's voice. "It's good to hear from you, Frances. All settled in?"

Frances took a deep breath and said, "Well, actually, no. I guess I did not understand the situation. I thought I was buying a house. Instead, it's a church! This is not what I expected. I'm not going to live in a church! So I'm coming back up to Atlanta and get back my money."

Mr. Whitehead's soft voice started with a slow drawl. "Now, Frances, we have already transferred the property to your name and wired the money to the owners. I can't believe you don't like the property. Just because it was a church at one time doesn't mean you can't live there. There is a lot of history with that property. Can't find places like that anymore. Why, here in Atlanta you would have paid four or five times more for that building alone, to say nothing of the land."

Frances tried to remain calm. "Yes, well, you can say nothing of the land. The part that is not swamp is a cemetery. The growth around the church is as high as my head. You can't even see the other buildings shown on the survey. And the church is full of junk—boxes and boxes of junk. Some of the junk is covered with sheets. You can only assume it is furniture or maybe just more junk."

"I know when you get through with the property, it will be a show place," Mr. Whitehead said cheerfully. "I hope the current heir doesn't find out what I let it go for. Good luck to you, Frances—I have another call."

Frances heard the sound of the telephone clicking off. Mary's voice came on the line almost immediately. "If you're finished with your call, the charges will be $4.73, including tax." Frances knew she had heard every word and this news would spread like wildfire.

Frances turned back to Doc and counted out the money Mary had said she owed for the call. She thanked him for letting her use his telephone, and he said she was welcome anytime she needed to make a call. "I hope I'll be seeing a lot of you in the future. Welcome to Synaxis," Doc said with a most friendly tone. Frances thanked him and turned to leave. But the thought of going back to the grocery store was more than she could bear. She knew, however, if she did not go back, she would be reduced to begging the cats for their food.

Opening the door to the grocery, she immediately heard, "Well, did ye make yer call?"

Frances walked to the counter and said, "Yes, thank you for helping me. I need to buy some food."

The little lady got to her feet and came up to the counter peering over her glasses. "We don't got a whole lot. Most folks grow their own and have cows and pigs. I'll see what we can do. You let me know what you use, and when I call for supplies, I can get what you need. A truck comes through here might near ever' week. I'll be glad to share what I got 'til we can get ya started. We can't let that little one go hungry.

Frances wondered what she meant by the "little one". She finally replied, "I came well prepared for them. They have at least a month's supply. I knew better than to let them run out of food. They can really throw a fit when they're hungry."

"They don't eat what you eat?"

"No, they beg for my food and try to take it away from me and I let them have part of it, but they still want their food."

"Hmmmm," the old lady replied, then walked around the room, telling Frances what she had available.

After Frances had settled her bill, placed her order, and loaded her car, she started back to face the music. She rehearsed all the way back to the church what she would tell the trio.

As soon as the car was out of sight, the door to the service station opened and a man in overalls hurried over to the grocery store. "Well, Doris, what'd she want?"

Doris stood at the front window, still watching the dust from the car going down the road. "Well, Sheriff, the more outside people I see, the more I wonder how they survive. It's a wonder they live to grow up. You wouldn't believe what she said 'bout feeding them babies. How many say was in the backseat?"

He looked down at the floor trying to think. "You couldn't really tell. They must've been in one of them contraptions they use to keep 'em safe. You couldn't rightly tell, but the backseat looked full."

When Frances arrived back at the church, she could hear three voices and see three sets of eyes at the kitchen window. She made her way back around to the front, vowing to find a way to get the back door open from the outside. When she opened the door to the kitchen from the hall, they were already at the door waiting for her.

Frances decided she would unload the car before filling them in on their predicament.

Chapter 3

Frances fixed her lunch and sat down at the table. Sitting at an adjacent table, the three cats watched for any indication that part of the food on her plate was for them. After the first bite, Frances started slowly, "Your Mama did not use the best judgment in planning how we were going to live. I took a small amount of the money to buy this place. I thought if we went to a small town, I would get more for our money. This place sounded like a good deal. We probably have enough money to last us two years. By that time, I should have a way to make some money. However, I did not think through what a person could do in a small town. Maybe if we could find enough stuff that has been stored here, we can sell part of it to make ends meet. Of course, we will have to find a nearby town where there is a greater market—namely a few people that have money to buy what we have to sell."

She could almost believe they were nodding their heads in agreement. "What would I do without you?"

After she had washed her dishes, she leaned against the sink and studied the room. Where would you start if you did not have a starting place? She decided that she would pull everything out of the pantry and put her personal belongings in there. Opening the door, she felt three brief brushes of fur going past her leg. Grabbing the first box, she tried to drag it into the kitchen, being careful not to block the door to the hallway.

After about two hours of backbreaking labor, she had the small room empty—except for three cats and three inches of dust. Thank goodness, she had brought a vacuum cleaner. After she had removed all the dust from the room, she decided that one of the covers in the kitchen could be used for a drape for the window, allowing two areas with privacy. When she uncovered the closest piece to her, she found a pretty chest beneath the cover. After she hung the cover over the window, she dragged the chest in front of the window. She would at least have a place to store her clothes.

Next, she decided to finish unloading her car. The trunk was so packed she wondered how she had managed to get as much as she did into such a small space. After arranging everything near the back door, she sat down to rest. She would have to lock the three cats in one of the rooms before opening the door to carry everything inside. Leaning her head back against the door, she stared at the beautiful trees. Closing her eyes, she listened to the birds singing and the gentle breeze in the leaves. If you did not know better, you would think you were in paradise. One bird was sitting on a high limb near the back door. Frances looked up to see what kind of bird was singing. As she peered past the trim of the door, she saw a small brass reflection on the ledge above the door. Standing up, she tried to reach the ledge, without success. Looking around, she spied a wooden bucket that would probably give her the extra few inches she needed. Holding on to the frame for support, she put her hand up and gripped the small brass object. "Hey, gang, we have a back door key." Only one small meow came back.

After she had established order to *her* room, she sat down in her chair in the kitchen and propped up her feet, hoping to come up with a master plan for survival. "We really need a bed. I don't think that table will work for much longer." She turned her head and looked at the corner behind her. There was a table against the wall that she might pad with some of the covers, which would do until she could find a bed with a mattress. Surely, in this mess, there was a bed. Counting the tables in the room, Frances decided she would stack all the boxes on top and under the tables to save space. She would save four of the tables to use for unpacking and sorting.

Walking over to the corner, she surveyed the area and the boxes. She decided the first thing she would do would be take enough of the covers off and take them outside to air so she could pad the table for a bed. Each time she removed a cover, one of the cats would investigate. What she found beneath the covers was startling. Every piece appeared to be museum quality. After a while, she ceased to gasp after each new find. Taking the covers outside to the fence, she spread them out in the sun. Hopefully, they would be aired before time for bed. *I will be like the princess and the pea*, she thought.

When she entered the kitchen, all three cats were either standing up on their hind legs and sniffing the pieces or sitting on top of a piece. If she could have interpreted their expressions, she imagined it would have been of pleasure. Dragging a large box over to one of the tables she had designated as a staging area, she opened the box and found about a dozen lampshades. "Well, kids, with all these shades, surely there are lamps. Has anyone found any lamps?" No reply. Putting the box beneath a storage table, she opened another box. In this box, she found some of the most exquisite linens she had ever seen. She tried to decide what price she could put on them if or when she decided to sell them. Next, she reached for a small box and ripped open the cord holding it closed. Inside this box was another wooden box. This box fit inside the outer box so tight that she had to virtually pry it out. Opening the inside wooden box, she almost fainted. "Oh my, what on earth have I found?" The box was full of sterling silver flatware. Picking up a spoon, she was amazed at the weight.

Frances carefully repacked the box and took it over to one of the storage tables. She sat down in her chair and looked around. In her mind, she calculated that the linens and silver alone would take care of her for several months. If every box and cover concealed the same treasurers as she had found this afternoon, what would the rest of the building provide? She sat still, feeling that if she moved she would wake up from some dream. Could it be possible that someone would actually sell this place full of antiques, not knowing what was here? "*Well, Mr. Attorney, you said a deal was a deal.* The deed had been registered and the check cashed. She couldn't go back.

The rest of the afternoon was spent opening boxes, often after having to remove cats from boxes so she could see the contents. She continued to be amazed at what she found. She was definitely going to have to make room to sort. The way the boxes and furniture were packed left little room to work. No wonder someone had just abandoned the place. Yet it would be interesting to find out what happened to the person who started the collection. She wondered how she could find out the history of this place. She also needed to find a way to determine the value of the pieces. *What I need is a computer*, she decided. "Did you guys see a computer shop when we came through town? I didn't think so. Don't you think, in view of what we have found this afternoon, we could buy a computer to start an inventory?" Sunshine looked at her and appeared to be giving his approval.

She went outside to gather the covers to take them inside. Standing at the fence, looking back at the church, she made a mental note of the things she needed to do. First, she needed to get someone to clear the growth from around the building. Second, she wanted a screened porch on the back so the babies could enjoy the outside. Third, she needed a way to do laundry. She could just sell a box to get the money. Actually, she didn't have to do that just yet. She could rely on her savings for a time.

When she folded the covers on the table/bed and put the sheets on top, the cats jumped in the middle and walked around, giving their approval. "Do you think you can rest now?" Each one flopped down and rolled over on their back to show their approval.

Frances lay down beside them and rubbed each in turn. "This is going to turn out fine. We have the place in the country we wanted, and there is even a small lake somewhere on the property. We don't have to worry about the cemetery. It will take care of itself. We have lots to keep us busy, and it doesn't look like I will have to leave home to get a job. Just short trips to sell a few items. We have just got to figure a way to organize what we have. We don't have to rush. Just take each day as it comes."

The next morning, after breakfast, Frances decided she needed to go through the entire building and look at the contents as much possible. Deciding that the cats could not get out of the building and they would come back to the kitchen when they got hungry, she opened the door to the hallway and stood staring at the long row of covers and boxes. The three cats came up beside her and looked up as if to say: "You mean we can have free run?"

Frances stood with her arms folded in the "I am to boss" stance. "Now, we have rules—when I call, you come. The first one that does not obey the rules will be put in the carrier until they know how to behave. Do we all understand?" The cats sat down and looked around and then at each other. They stood and down the narrow path they went, one behind the other, their tails high in the air.

Frances counted the doors on each side of the hallway and found there were five on each side. She decided she could have ten storage areas to group items. All the large pieces could go in the sanctuary. Her major problem was how to find room to sort the items. If she took half of the money she planned to live on for the next two years, she could build a garage on the other side of the porch and have someone work part time to help her with the heavy pieces. Frances did not want to start selling pieces until she could educate herself on the value of what she had. Perhaps she could hire an appraiser to help. Suddenly, Frances was afraid she was going too fast. What if she spent her money and had nothing left to live on? She knew she had to get a telephone and she was sure that was going to cost a lot since it appeared no lines had ever been run to the property.

Going back to the kitchen, she decided she needed to go into town and make some inquiries. She unpacked some clothes and got towels to bathe before making her trip. Then she went to the door to the hall and called the cats. Like little soldiers, they came marching back in the same order in which they had left. Tails still high in the air. The only difference was that cobwebs coated their whiskers. Closing the door, she told them she would be back soon. "I'm going to find someone to build you a porch so you can go outside and enjoy the weather." They had already started washing their faces with their paws.

Chapter 4

Frances decided her first stop would be the hardware store. They would know about carpenters and could perhaps recommend someone. Finding a place to buy a computer would be another problem. As she opened the door to the hardware, a pleasant woman coming from the back of the store greeted her, "Can I help you?"

"I want to make some additions and I need a carpenter. Do you know anyone that would be qualified?" Frances said a silent prayer, as the clerk paused for only a moment before replying, "It'd depend on what ya want. If it doesn't require a lot of finishing work, we got someone local that could do a good job. If you want a lot of trim and detailed work, you'll have to find someone perhaps in Marshland 'bout ten miles from here."

After Frances explained what she wanted, the lady said, "I reckon the Morris boys would do just fine. I say boys—they're in the sixties, but everybody still calls 'em the boys. They live on the next street behind the store. If you like, we can walk out back and cut across the alley. I can introduce you. Let me put a sign in the window." She walked to the front and put up sign that said: "Gone out." As she came back toward Frances, she said,

"Everyone just writes down what they get if I'm not here—don't have to worry 'bout locking the door. I've never had a problem. My name's Nadine."

"I'm Frances. I recently bought some property just outside town," Frances explained. She thought to herself that Nadine probably knew already, but she would tell her anyway.

They went through a gate and started around the house, following a brick path. Frances was looking at the beautiful trim and lines of the old home. It obviously had been well cared for. There was no comparison to the stores. "Do the Morris boys live here?" Frances asked as she was taking in every detail of the house.

Nadine laughed and said, "No, this is where I live. It's convenient to the store. Most of the store owners live behind their stores on this street. All we have to do is run across the alley to get home. The Morris boys live in front of me."

The front yard was as pretty as the back, with lots of large trees and flowers. Frances looked up and down the lawns at the other homes. All were beautiful with large porches wrapping around the front and sides. It was like stepping into another world. The street was not wide, but both sides were nearly identical, with carefully maintained homes. If someone had told Frances two days ago that Synaxis had another face besides the one seen by anyone passing through town on the highway, she would not have believed it. She did not realize she had stopped and was in her own little world until Nadine spoke. "Oh good, they're home."

Sittings on the front porch in rockers were two identical-looking men. They both had white hair and twinkling blue eyes. Each wore a smile, and as Nadine and Frances approached, they stood and the one on the right said, "Well, Nadine, it's so good to have you visit with us today. Who do you have with you?" Nadine turned and said, "This is Frances. She bought the old church property and wants some work done. You think y'all would have time to help her?"

The other man said, "Really depends on what ya want. Don't know if we'd like to spend much time out there. People 'round here don't go out there much. Although we sure could use a change—just about run out of anything to do around here."

Frances explained her plan to add to the back and asked how much they thought it would cost. She told them she did not have a lot of money, that most of it had been spent buying the place. She was hoping they wouldn't think she was a rich lady they could take advantage of.

The first man looked at his brother and said, "If you can pay for the material, we'll work by the hour. I say it shouldn't take more'n a week or two. Don't think it'll run much and you can pay us a little along if you don't have it all up front."

Frances was astonished. "I appreciate that, but it won't be necessary. I had a little left over after I paid for the property. When could you start?"

The first man looked at his watch and then his brother. "I think we just have time to get to the lumberyard today. I'm sure Nadine's got the nails, screen, and other stuff we need. We'll be there right after the sun comes up in the morning."

Frances could not believe her luck. Things were going too easy. She reached over and took each man's hand, saying, "I'll have a pot of coffee."

As she and Nadine went back across the street, Frances said, "Thank you, Nadine. They are wonderful. Since you did such a good job with my addition, what can be done about a helping me find a computer and a telephone?"

Nadine laughed and said, "Those are easy. Let's stop at my house and I can make some calls."

As they entered the front door, Frances could not believe the architecture and furnishings. Nadine led Frances down a wide entrance hall to a cheerful room with bright sofas and chairs. She offered Frances a chair and brought them a glass of iced tea. Then, picking up the telephone, she said, "Mary, our new neighbor needs a telephone. When ya think Ben can run the line?" Listening for a few moments, she turned and said, "Mary thinks they have all the materials, and if nothing goes wrong, he can start in the morning. She said she only has four jacks and four phones on hand. If you need more, she'll have to order them." Turning back to the phone, she said, "Mary, while you're on the line, connect me with Mark over in Marshland."

After a few moments, Nadine said into the phone, "Mark, this is Nadine. Our new neighbor needs a computer." Turning to Frances with the phone still to her ear, she told her what he had in stock and Frances made her choice.

After Nadine hung up the telephone, she told Frances that Mark would bring it home with him that evening, and she would have the Morris boys bring it out in the morning. She told her she could just pay for it when she paid for the materials they picked up at her store.

"What else do you need to get you set up? When is the moving van going to deliver your furniture? The sheriff, who knows everyone that comes and goes, said he hadn't seen anyone looking like they didn't know where they were going."

Frances explained to Nadine that she wasn't bringing any furniture with her. The property came furnished and she would just use what was there. Then she suddenly remembered, "I do need a washer and a dryer. I'll probably need a mattress set when I find the bed, but I can't buy that until I know what size." Looking over her glass of tea, she saw Nadine's eyes widen. Suddenly thinking how funny that must have sounded, she said, "You would not believe the mess the place is in. Everything is either covered with sheets or in boxes. I've been using some of the sheets folded on top of a table to sleep on. I expect everything I need is probably there somewhere—I just need to find it. That's why I'm planning to build a garage, so I'll have a place to put things so they can be sorted. I'm going to need help getting things sorted. I'm living in a large room that was probably used as a kitchen, and fortunately, there's limited plumbing in another of the rooms, which is large enough for the washer and dryer, I think."

Jumping up, Nadine said, "Look at my washer and dryer and see if they're what you want. If so, we can call Ron and have him bring them home tonight."

Frances was delighted and the call was made to Ron who said they could bring them out tonight and he would bring what plumbing supplies were needed. Frances again leaned back in the cushions and shook her head in disbelief. Looking at her watch, she said she really had to get back home; she had promised she would not be gone long. Nadine asked, "Children?"

Going out the door, Frances turned and smiled. "No, just three stubborn cats."

Frances caught herself smiling all the way back home. Suddenly, she realized that she already thought of it as going home, not back to the church. She was giddy with excitement when she parked her car. Stepping out, she hugged herself and then danced around the car. "I'm home!"

The three cats were sitting in the window, staring out at her performance. Zeus looked at Star and Sunshine and in their language decided either the stress had gotten to her or she had gotten drunk while she was gone. They could not decide which they preferred. They did like the big smile she had on her face as she came running up the back steps. Opening the door, she cried, "Everything is wonderful! It can't get any better! We are in paradise!" The three cats peering over their shoulders at her communicated to each other in unison, "Drunk."

Frances was still dancing around the room in happiness. The cats had moved from the window to the tables and were jumping from table to table, following her around as if waiting for something to happen. Finally, she sat down and told them all about her afternoon. They stared at her as if they understood every word. Probably, they were waiting for her to finally wind down and feed them. Frances finished her story and stood. "We're going to celebrate tonight. You are going to eat off real china plates. You're going to have extra treats, and I just might find you a crystal bowl for your water." Each cat, liking all this celebrating, nodded in approval.

Frances was sitting in her chair, making a list of things she needed to do and watching the cats wash their faces after their celebration when each cat's ears perked up and they started turning their heads to listen. Running to their favorite vantage point, they watched the procession coming around the driveway. In the first truck was her new washer and dryer, the second held boxes she assumed contained the computer, and there was a large truck loaded with lumber, plus two cars.

The cats watched anxiously as everyone got out of their vehicles. Frances told the cats to stay back from the door as everyone came in. Doris, Nadine, and someone else were carrying picnic baskets. The men were unloading the washer and dryer and the boxes. Everyone was laughing and talking at the same time. Doris said, "You haven't met Peggy or Ron and Mark." Each one came up and gave her a welcome.

Peggy called out, "We brought food, we want to have a party." At the word *food*, the three cats looked out from beneath the table.

"Let me get some linens for the table," Frances said as she headed for the box she had found earlier. As she spread out the long linen cloth and placed napkins on the table, she saw eyebrows go up and side glances. Immediately, the sound of happy voices returned and large containers of food were placed in the middle of the table. Doris said they brought disposable plates and utensils so as not to have to clean up afterwards.

The men headed to the room Frances indicated would be the location for the washer and dryer. The Morris boys said they were going to leave their truck and unload it in the morning. They could ride home with Doris. Mark was positioning the computer on the table Frances wanted to use until she could come up with a better location. The cats' ears perked up again, but they did not leave the spot under the table/bed for fear of being trampled. Another car was coming up beside the rest. Nadine looked out and called out, "Come on in, Doc, and Doris Two."

The two came in carrying cakes. Nadine said, "You know Doc and this is Doris Two, his wife."

The pretty petite blond came up and greeted Frances, making her feel as if they had known each other for years.

"We are so glad you came to live here. We know you are just going to love it," Doris said. Frances noticed, as Doris was giving everyone orders as to where to put food and look for chairs, that Doris did not have the accent she had used on her first visit to her store.

"Doris, you sound different," Frances observed.

Grinning, Doris said she used the accent when strangers came into town. It discourages people from hanging around long. "Gives us time to decide if we want to keep them."

Frances stared at the group that had gathered around and added, "Well, since you are all here, I guess it means I get to stay."

About that time, a siren was heard coming up the drive. Following the car with the siren was a utility truck. The sheriff was carrying a large brown sack and the man from the utility truck was carrying a large cooler. The woman with him was carrying a gallon jug of iced tea. By this time, the cats were no longer peering out; they were as far back against the wall as they could get and huddled together for protection. The woman came briskly over and said, "I guess you have already figured out that I am Mary and this is Ben. He could not wait to get started and we heard there was a party."

Frances could not believe that the kitchen had been turned into such a festive gathering. Down each side of the long table were assorted styles of chairs. Someone had even put candelabra, complete with candles, in the center of the table. Everyone found a chair and Doc said, "Let's have a prayer before we begin." Each person joined hands with the person next to them and he began,

"Lord, we thank you for all the blessings you have brought to us. A special thanks for the new member we have added to our family and may she learn to love us as much as we will love her. We would be remiss if we did not mention all the wonderful food you have allowed us to have, and we pray it will strengthen our bodies so we can continue our work for you. Amen."

Frances repeated, "Amen!"

After they finished eating, the women cleared the table and the men set out to their respective tasks. One of the Morris boys helped Mark with the wiring necessary for the computer and the other helped Ron and the sheriff with the washer/dryer installation. Doc was helping Ben try to find the best places to put the telephone, where she could get to it as easily as possible. They had already decided that might not be such an easy task.

Ron came out and asked Frances where the hot water storage unit was located. Frances turned around in the room and stared at the four walls. She could not remember ever seeing a hot water heater. She had only turned on the water, and after it cleared up from standing in the pipes so long, she'd had hot water. Stopping to think about where it was coming from did not occur to her. She had been too happy to care. "I really don't remember seeing it. Of course, I've not looked in any of the other rooms."

The Morris boy helping Mark said, "It looks to me like the pipe is coming from downstairs. Would've been difficult to run it beneath the floor to another part of the building. Where's the door going downstairs?"

Again, Frances had not seen any door that would have gone downstairs. "I haven't spent too much time in the sanctuary. I would think it's probably located at the front."

Everyone had smiles and high spirits again. They were headed for another adventure. Frances had never seen a group enjoy life as much. Everyone started down the hallway in single file. As a man would come to a door off the hall, he would select it as one of his assignments and crawl over boxes and covered furniture to go inside the room. The women went straight to the sanctuary to start their search. Every light in the building had been turned on. The cats made their way over to the door at the kitchen and peered down the hallway at the sight, but not one ventured to follow the parade.

Doris and Peggy stood just inside the door of the sanctuary and debated on the best way to go along the wall to see if a doorway was blocked. Doris decided she would crawl over the top and peer down. She produced a small penlight from her pocket, looked around for something to step on to get on top, and off she went on her knees. Frances stood there and realized something. Doris wasn't such an old woman. As a matter of fact, she was very attractive. What had happened to change her since the previous time Frances had seen her at the store?

Doris Two was coaching Peggy at one side of the room near the front door and Nadine was on the other side of the room. The men were rearranging boxes and furniture to make small aisles through the middle of the room where a person could make their way around. Doc called out to Frances that he had found a stack of bed frames. Mark and Ron went toward the direction of his voice, and after a brief discussion, the men decided on which frame to try to get out and the best way without the aid of a crane. Ron and Mark crawled up on top of the surrounding pieces and lifted them out of the hole. The sheriff and Ben slid down the small aisle and held it above their heads as they carried it all the way to the kitchen. The Morris boys were right behind them warning of obstacles and cautioning them to be careful.

Doris called out at the front of the sanctuary that she could see two doors. All the men hurried back to the closest point they could get to her and started moving everything so they could have another path over to her. She sat perched on a high object and gave directions on the easiest route to take. After struggling with everything, they finally arrived at the first door. Clearing a place large enough for the door to open, someone reached inside to find a light. The door opened into what proved to be a storage area. Perhaps it had been used for an office. Back to the shuffling of boxes and furniture, they finally arrived at the other door.

When the path was large enough, the door was opened, and the sheriff announced they had hit pay dirt. As he led the procession with his large flashlight, everyone made their way down the wooden steps. A pull chain at the top of the stairs had lit up a bulb that could at its best be compared to a candle. Everyone was walking as lightly as possible, making hardly any sound. Certain boards would creak as someone stepped on the particular board. The sheriff reached up to a string and pulled on another light. Again, a small glow lit the area near the light. The sheriff swept the beam of his flashlight around the room and everyone stared a rows and rows of wooden crates.

Frances said in a low voice, "More stuff."

Someone else said, "Yes."

When they were all standing of the floor of the basement, Ron turned around in a circle to get his bearings. Someone reached over and pulled another string to the usual light. At least the walkways were wider and they would find additional strings to pull along the way. Finally, at the back of the room, everyone stood looking up at the pipes. After a few minutes, Mark said they should work their way over to the corner beneath the bathroom. The pipe running over to the place where the sink was located was the only direction any plumbing was going. In the corner, they found a large ancient water heater. Mark lit up the floor around the bottom of the heater and said he was surprised something this old did not leak. He would guess it was because it had not been used very much.

The women left the men to plan how they were going to do the plumbing and went back up to the kitchen. Nadine told Frances she did not see a pry bar downstairs, but that she was ready to start opening the crates she had one in the store. Frances said it would probably be a long time before she could start on the lower level.

Peggy cried with excitement, "Look, the Morris boys made room for your bed." Standing over near the table where Frances slept was a magnificent bed that had been put up and was ready for a mattress set. "Ron can bring home a set tomorrow, and if you don't have sheets, I got a nice shipment in a few weeks ago," Peggy volunteered.

Frances said, "If I have any, I would not know where to find them."

Frances stood staring at the European lacquer bed decorated with chinoiseries, the four posters rising almost to the high ceiling. The cats were still making their normal inspection stance on their hind legs with noses in the air, sniffing the addition to the room. "You will think you are wealthy when you start sleeping on this bed. That means you will have to act as if you are wealthy and develop a few manners," Frances told the cats.

Nadine stood up to get a better look and immediately let out a low, "Oh, how cute. They are beautiful. No wonder you love them so much." This prompted everyone else to stand to get a look at the evasive cats. The cats stopped their inspection of the furniture and turned to stare in return. The room was quiet as each party participated in the cats' game "you will blink first." The sound of clank, clank of the pipes in the bathroom sent them back to the safety spot under the sleeping table.

The Morris boys came through the room on their way to the laundry room. They glanced at the bed and then at Frances with a sheepish smile. They were obviously proud of their fast job. In a few minutes, one of them started using a drill to cut through the floor and called out that they were going to lower a pipe through the hole to them. One of them would call out they were bringing down some fittings and tools.

Doris Two asked Frances how on earth she was going to sort out all the contents of the building. "That is why I'm having a garage built on the back. I plan to move the contents of several rooms to the garage and do the sorting there, then move the contents back to a room designated for that category. I'm going to start a database to inventory the items so values can be placed on them and I can find buyers." Doris asked how she was going to do all that work alone. "I guess I'll have to hire someone to help. For no other reason, to keep me from going crazy trying to cope."

Frances saw four women looking at each other, then as if by a signal, Doris started to speak. "We want to apply for the job."

Frances was flabbergasted. "Why on earth would you want to apply?"

Doris continued speaking for the group. "We are bored. We never have a challenge. We would work for free just to have something to do."

"What about your businesses?" Peggy chimed in.

"James takes care of them when we're busy. If someone wants something, they just go pick it up and take the money to James. Everyone in town knows where the keys are hid to the back doors, and it is pretty well an honor system."

Frances thought she could never find a better deal than this and could not think of any reason to refuse the help. She could pay them by giving them items they admired as payment for services, and it would solve a lot of her problems. They obviously knew a lot about the value and would be a great asset to her.

"I know you probably thought I was crazy when I came to town, so I don't want to do anything that would confirm your beliefs. When can we start?"

Chapter 5

Frances was amazed at the speed the construction was taking. At the end of the second day, the Morris boys had the screened porch finished. She found out their names were Sam and Otis. They said those cats needed to have a place where they could watch the progress. They felt sorry for them having to sit crowded up in that window to see what was going on. The three cats had overcome their fright of the noise and would lie on the floor looking at every board that was laid for the garage and every nail that was driven. Each morning, they would position themselves on the sunny side of the porch and take their morning bath.

At the end of the second week, Frances was working on the computer when the cats ran into the kitchen, then to the bathroom window and finally back to the porch. Frances knew something special must be happening. She had been hearing the sound of the hammers on the roof of the garage, but they had stopped. She could hear the crying of the cats on the porch and then she heard the sound of a car headed into the woods toward the cemetery. As she walked out onto the porch, she saw the car coming out into the clearing. The cats were running around each other and crying. "Don't act so happy! You're supposed to be mad at him." Frances recognized the car the minute she saw it. She stepped outside with the determination he would not be invited inside. Evidently, he saw her because the car turned in her direction before heading back out.

As the car door opened and he stepped out, she said with a small hint of sarcasm. "Well, this is certainly a surprise. We don't see many city folks around these parts. What brought you to this part of the country?"

Joseph came toward her, glancing at the cats that were still doing their dance and standing on their hind legs crying through the screen. "I wasn't sure if you were doing all right and thought I'd take a few days off to see if you needed anything."

Frances folded her arms and leaned back against a tree. After a short silence, she said, "You weren't too concerned about my needing anything when you were trying to settle. As a matter of fact, I thought you wouldn't have enough money to buy gas after the pitiful story you told. I will repeat again, what do you want?" By this time, she saw that Sam and Otis had come down from the roof and had sat down not far away, as if to say, "If you need us, just let us know."

At the same time, she heard another car coming up the lane. She glanced up and saw the sheriff's car going toward the cemetery and stopping just before entering the woods. In a few minutes, two more cars followed him. Joseph looked at the group parked at a distance and asked, "Are they going to have a funeral? I don't see a hearse."

Frances gave a slow smile. "Maybe they're waiting to see if there's going to be a body."

Joseph frowned slightly and then, as if to show he understood, revealed an embarrassed smile. He walked over to the door and went out onto the porch. All three cats were competing to see who was going to get more of his attention. He stooped and was rubbing them and told them he had missed them very much. Sam and Otis stood up and walked out of the yard toward the cars. Frances assumed they were going to report to the vigilante group who had arrived.

Frances was sure Joseph could never understand the friendships she had developed since her arrival at her new home. Joseph stood and looked around. "Is this where you're living? It isn't exactly what I expected."

Frances thought to herself it wasn't what she had expected, either, but said, "I was able to get it cheap." She stood in her same spot and was determined not to invite him inside. He was picking up each cat in turn and holding them close to his chest and rubbing their heads. Frances would tell the cats they could sleep on the floor tonight as punishment for betraying her.

After a few minutes, Joseph said, "I see you're building quite an addition, a three-car garage. You must have a lot of plans."

Frances glanced at the building and said she needed the space for storage. She had accumulated a lot since she had bought the property. Joseph looked at her and she knew he was wondering what on earth was going on. He knew she had very little money when she came here and she did not appear to have a job. She could see him glancing toward the open door, but chose to ignore the gesture. She knew his curiosity was getting the best of him.

Joseph seemed to be searching for something to say. Finally, he said, "Very unusual country. You must be lonely. The people in town don't seem very friendly. I filled the gas tank and the attendant even wrote down my license number. When I asked how to get to your address, he acted as if he didn't want to tell me." Joseph's manners did not permit him to sit without being asked, and he just continued holding one cat after the other.

Frances finally broke the silence. "Joseph, I do not know why you made this long trip. You were the one who asked for the divorce. You are the one who felt like we no longer had anything in common. You gave me what you felt you could spare from our marriage and sent me on my way. I have nothing left to give."

Joseph stood silently for a few minutes. Finally, he put down the cat and came back outside. "I wanted to make sure you were okay. Everything happened so fast and you left town without as much as a good-bye. I called your attorney to find out where you were living and was surprised that you had totally left your familiar surroundings to go somewhere without friends or family. I should have known you were a strong person—a survivor. I just had to see for myself."

Frances looked away. "I didn't think you would care where I went. I didn't feel any need to tell anyone. I thought if I had to start my life over, I would do it without everyone watching and waiting to see if I failed. I am so sorry you had to come so far. If you had written, I would have told you I'm fine, and I really am. I enjoy this place, the peace, and its history. The people are very nice once you get to know them. If you want to know, that is half the town down by the trees waiting to see if I am all right. The man at the service station is the sheriff. The other two cars are three sisters and the wife of the pharmacist. They have been so much help. I did not know that people existed as good as them. They have restored a faith in me that I didn't think existed. If you told me a year ago I would be this content outside my life with you, I would not have believed you. I am sorry you had to make such a long trip, but you did get to see the cats. They obviously miss you."

Joseph looked at the ground for a long time before saying anything. "I think I'll drive over to the coast for a while. It will do me good to get away. I don't have a lot of time to think at home. I work a lot, go home to bed, get up the next morning, and start over. Walking on the sand barefooted will help clear my head. Thank you for seeing me and letting me pet the cats." He looked back at the trio sitting quietly, side by side. They were looking at him with a gaze that only Frances understood. Joseph reached over, patted her shoulder, and turned to go to his car. He opened the door and stood for several moments with his hand on the knob, looking at her, before getting in and driving off.

Frances stood a long time still leaning against the tree. She watched his car go back down the lane. She then turned and walked back inside without looking at the group at the clearing. She went down the hall to the sanctuary and sat down on a pew that had been cleared. The three cats came in silently and climbed up next to her. She gathered them close and began to cry. The tears dropped on their backs, but they didn't move to lick them off. After a while, she heard the engines of the cars start and the cars driving back down the lane without stopping. She heard Sam and Otis's truck leave. The tears kept coming. She realized this was the first time she had allowed herself to cry since the day Joseph announced his plans for the divorce. "Well, babies, Mama is finally alive again. I'm starting to feel pain." She could hear the soft purrs of the cats, but they did not move.

Chapter 6

The next morning, Frances woke to the sound of a truck coming up the lane. The cats were piled around her in their usual spot. When she opened her eyes and saw the clock, she realized that she did not have her usual pot of coffee ready. All four jumped up, making ready for the day. Frances ran into the closet and jumped into a work outfit, brushed her teeth, and had the coffee started before Sam and Otis had made it inside. When she looked out the kitchen window while running the coffee water, she saw them standing in front of the garage looking up and discussing how to finish the top. She opened the door and the cats ran out in front of her to say their good mornings to the two men.

"Coffee will be ready in a few minutes. I got a late start." Sam and Otis nodded and smiled.

She heard another car coming up the lane and saw Sam and Otis raise their hands in a wave. The car pulled up to the back and four women got out with baskets and announced that they needed to eat breakfast before anyone started work. Frances was so glad to see her friends. She went back inside to get placemats and napkins for the table on the porch. When she turned and started back for plates and flatware, she noticed the cats, all three tails up in the air, and they were winding around everyone's ankles, sniffing the air.

After everyone had enjoyed the food, Sam and Otis picked up their caps to go to work. The women took the dishes inside, and after everything was cleared, Peggy said, "Where do we start?"

All of them stood looking from one to the other. Finally, they laughed and started clearing a place to work. They decided they would use the tables in the kitchen for the time to sort and start a database. Several of the tables had been grouped near the door to the hall and several had been placed on the back wall. They decided they would do a quick sort first and then refine their inventory later. Nadine was elected to take care of the computer. First, they carried and dragged the contents of the hall outside the kitchen, along with the first room down the hall, into kitchen.

By noon, most of the boxes had been opened and inspected. At first, the work was slow. No one could not believe the beautiful items they removed from the boxes. But after a couple of hours, they had adjusted to the surprises and the work became routine. Occasionally, all work stopped for a special find.

Frances was glad there was no mention of the previous day. At lunch, they ate sandwiches from the fixings in the refrigerator and rested on the porch for a few minutes. Frances said she was glad it had been finished and all meals could be served there, so as not to have to use the valuable space in the kitchen for eating. Sam said he thought they should clear out two rooms near the kitchen and remove a partition to make a place to put her bed and a place for her to have some privacy. A general debate was held as to where to store the items until they could make progress and how to manage the work. Otis said the floor of the garage was to be poured the next day, and they could have the roof finished to a point where it would be waterproof. Peggy drew up a flowchart of how they could bring items out and put them on certain tables for documentation in the computer before taking them to the garage for sorting and then back to the area designated for that particular type of inventory. Nadine and Doris thought it would be easier to purchase folding tables for the garage than build them. Sam said that when they were finished, the tables could be given to the school. Frances agreed that they would be a business expense and that would benefit the school as well.

The afternoon seemed to fly by. No one could believe the progress that had been made. They had cleared everything out of four rooms. Frances barely had room to get to her bed. The entire back wall was piled high with boxes. They had done some sorting in the kitchen, putting like items together. They had labeled the outside of the boxes with descriptions of the items inside for quick reference.

Chapter 7

The next day, Frances was working alone at the computer. The team had decided to catch up on their personal work, and after the floor was ready, they could start back to work. Nadine had ordered the tables and they should be delivered soon. Everything was quiet. Frances assumed the cats were napping on the porch. Sam and Otis had overseen the pouring of the concrete and were on the roof, trying to decide on something.

Frances heard their footsteps hurrying down the ladder and onto the porch. Sam came through the door first. He was walking fast and turned his head to look at her as he passed. His eyes were large and he did not say a word. Right behind him was Otis, same expression, same speed. She leaned back in her chair and listened as they headed through the hall in almost a run. She heard their fast hushed talking in the sanctuary. She could hear boxes and furniture being moved and more low voices. She turned her head and tried to hear what was being said. All she could hear was "Hurry." After a few minutes, she heard, "It has to be here somewhere."

Frances got out of her chair and walked toward the door. When she went into the sanctuary, she saw the two men at the front of the building frantically looking behind the stacks at the wall. Otis was up on top directing Sam. She came right up to them before either noticed her. "What is wrong?"

Both men looked as if they had seen a ghost. Sam spoke first. "You better go outside and look up." Frances walked to the front door and went out on the porch. Sam came up behind her. "Walk out and look up at the roof."

Frances went down the steps and turned to look up. There in the belfry were all three cats. Star and Zeus were sitting across from each other with their heads back enjoying the breeze. Sunshine was on one other edge, trying to reach across the expanse to grab the short rope attached to the bell. The rope was waving in the breeze and it looked as if he was going to leap to it at any moment. Frances shouted, "Get down from there this instant!"

All three cats came over to the edge nearest her and peered down. "How did you get up there?" Star turned and jumped down from the ledge to the inside of the belfry. Sam called to Otis to try to see where she came into the sanctuary.

Sunshine made gestures as if he was going to jump down onto the top of the roof. Frances called for him to stop and was glad Zeus decided to follow Star. She knew Sunshine would follow the rest. She and Sam went back into the building and closed the door. Star sat just inside the door washing her feet. She had the usual cobwebs in her whiskers. Zeus came out into the opening with his tail and head lowered. Otis said he could see a small opening in the wall and a crack that was probably a door that went to the stairs. Sunshine came out from the stacks of boxes and looked up with his usual expression. "Aren't you ashamed? You scared Sam and Otis. What are they going to think of your behavior?" Frances scolded.

Sam and Otis assured her it was all right. "We should know they can take care of themselves, and we were told they got into a lot of mischief. We were just afraid they might fall." Sam laughed. "I could just see that big yellow cat jumping and holding on to that rope." Otis caught up in the laughter. "Everyone around would come running when they heard that bell ringing. They would think something was wrong."

Frances could not help smiling. She placed her hands on her hips in her position of authority and said, "Okay, you had your fun. You get back to the porch and don't do that again." The three stood and made their usual parade, with Star in front.

As Frances, Sam, and Otis got back to the kitchen, she heard a truck coming up the lane. Sam and Otis looked at each other. Sam was first to speak. "We forgot to mention we asked J. T. to come out and bring some of his equipment." Otis chimed in, "We thought it would speed up things for you a little."

Frances walked out on the porch to see a truck pulling up with what looked like farm equipment on the back. A man got out of the truck and three teenage boys followed. He walked up to Sam and Otis and shook hands. "I brought my sons, Don, Kevin, and Jason, to help." Frances looked from person to person and asked, "Help with what?"

The boys were already unloading some of the equipment. J. T. replied, "Why, clean up the yard." The first piece of equipment started with loud noises. One of the boys was standing on the back and off around the house he went. The other son was soon on his piece of equipment headed around the other side. The cats were running from side to side watching the work.

The only comment they offered was, "We hope you don't mind. We know you admired our yards, and we thought if you could start seeing some results, you would be happier."

They had gone back inside and were headed for the first two rooms on the left of the hall. They had tape measurers out and were tapping on the walls and listening. "I know it would be nice, but how expensive are these people?" Frances asked.

Sam looked at her. "J. T. said if he could have a nice gift for his wife, that's all the pay he needed. She would love something for her house and we didn't think you would mind."

Frances shook her head in disbelief. "You two really know how to barter. Is there anything you cannot arrange?"

"We can't seem to decide the best way to arrange this room to make that bed look good," Otis said, a serious look on his face. "We want the door to be situated at the best location."

The three of them walked from room to room and then came up with the best solution. Sam thought it would be best to move the entrance to the pantry to the bedroom and they wanted to take part of the bathroom and make another bath for the bedroom. After several sketches on a box, they all agreed on a floor plan.

The next day, Sam and Otis brought another load of lumber. When Frances went outside, they were unloading it in the garage. She could just see all her money going out. She knew she would have to get busy selling some of the inventory in a hurry. She did not want to hurt their feelings, but was also worried. "What are we doing now?" she asked in her most cheery voice.

They both replied together, "Shelves—it will help us organize."

When Frances took them their second cup of coffee, she could not believe their progress. They could do more work without looking busy than anyone she had ever seen. All the lumber was already laid out, stacked near the saw, with markings on it where to cut. Each of them took their cup of coffee and turned to stare at the wall. She took her cup and stood staring with them. After two sips of coffee, the men sat down their cups without a word and turned to the saw. Frances stepped back and watched. In a few minutes, all the lumber with marks had been cut. Each man was picking up a piece with one hand and getting their hammers the other with the other. Walking over to the wall, they started nailing. In what seemed like another few minutes, shelves were covering one end of the garage. Frances could only turn and walk back inside in amazement.

She had only been at her computer for a few minutes when they came inside carrying tools. Their only comment was, "We're fixing to make a mess." They went inside the first room and closed the door. Frances could hear the sound of power saws and lumber being pried loose. In an hour, the door opened, and the two men came out carrying lumber. She went to the room and was surprised to find the dividing wall was already removed. She could not believe how little mess was left. You could barely see where the partition had been. Evidently, it had been added after the original room had been built. The cats came in to make their usual inspection. They walked along the floor, sniffing the place where the wall had been, jumped into each window, and looked out to see what was outside and then looked at the walls. She walked over to a window and looked outside. She could not believe the transformation of the yard. What had been filled with vegetation almost as high as her head was now cut low. J. T. had assured her that in a few weeks, the grass would start growing and the brown that was showing from lack of sunlight would disappear.

She turned and walked outside, going into the area that she had thought was a small garden when she arrived. The hedges were trimmed to maintain the privacy of the area. The bench and birdbath gave the area a peaceful feeling. She walked over to the birdbath and saw that flowers had been planted. The front of the building also hosted new flowers. The blooms gave her a feeling of appreciation for all the work that had been done to help her. She walked up the lane toward the cemetery, looking at the area with a new vision. She stopped to look at the names on the stones. Some were so old one could barely read them. She looked up at the beautiful trees and the shrubs that had probably been planted with love in years past. She saw stones for small babies and stones for old people. She stopped to listen to the singing of the birds and heard herself saying aloud, "As soon as I get organized and sell some of the inventory, I will use part of the money to restore you to your beauty."

Walking back to the house, she saw the car pull into the back with her four new friends. She hastened her pace, and when they saw her coming, they threw up their hands in a friendly gesture.

Doris exclaimed in a loud voice, "You're not picking out a place for yourself, are you?" Everyone chimed in with laughter.

After they sat down in the chairs around the table on the porch, a new sound came from inside the house. All three cats came out the door of the kitchen at the same time, with ears back and their claws trying to get a grip on the slick boards. They headed over to a corner where a box was sitting and darted behind. The only problem was there was not enough room for all three cats and the back end of Zeus and Sunshine were sticking out from each side. All five women jumped up at the same time, asking, "What on earth?" They followed the sound inside to the new bedroom. Sam was using a sander to remove the finish from the floor. The beautiful old boards were already showing his progress.

Otis stopped glazing the windows and told them in a loud voice, "It would cost a fortune to put wood like this in a home now." Nadine picked up a piece of sandpaper and walked over to where the partition had been removed and started sanding the seam that was left. Frances picked up another piece and started on the other wall. Doris and Peggy found the can of spackling and knife and came behind them, sealing the holes left by the nails when the partition was put up originally.

Even though the room was large, everyone kept bumping into each other. Sam was the only one who could get around without hitting someone. When you heard him coming, you naturally moved over. In record time, the room was ready for paint on the walls and varnish on the floor. Otis said that would have to wait for the next day. Everyone lined up at the sink to wash off the grime from the project. Doris turned her head and listened. "Do I hear a car?"

Someone looked out. "It's Ron and Mark—correction, it's Ron and Mark, followed by the sheriff." The three men came in carrying buckets of chicken and jugs of ice tea. Another sack held all the trimmings.

Doris told the sheriff, "You sure have a nose for food. If you had a nose for crime like you have for food, we could send you to New York and make a fortune."

He revealed his slow grin. "Well, I always make fresh tea every morning and put it in the refrigerator at the station. When I smell food going by, I grab my jugs and follow the car. Can I help it if no one in this town can remember to buy tea when they shop?"

Ron leaned back. "Why should we waste our money? We just wave a chicken leg out the window and you follow us like a stray puppy."

Frances felt sorry from him when everyone was laughing. "You come out here anytime you feel like eating. I don't like to eat alone, and I will share whatever I can keep away from the cats." At the word *cats*, all three decided they had been invited and came out from hiding to see if anyone would have mercy and give them a bite.

After everyone had finished, the sheriff said he thought he had turned at the wrong lane. The place was really looking good. He was going to have to start checking the progress every day to make sure he did not miss anything. He wandered inside and checked out the room they had worked on that day.

After a while, Frances went to make sure he was not sick and found him in the new room with a paint roller. He had half the walls finished. He stopped and looked over his shoulder. "Someone else can take a small brush and do the trimming. It doesn't take long to get the middle, and if I move around, it will shake down the food and I can dig into that pie I saw in the refrigerator." Frances walked around the room, staring at the transformation. She could not believe it could be so pretty and could not wait until draperies and furniture were installed.

When she went back to the porch, she asked Nadine if she had brought the bills for the materials. Nadine produced a folder with a neat invoice itemizing each item that had been purchased and where it had been used. Frances eyes went down the page, and when she got to the bottom, she saw there was only a 10 percent charge added to the material. "You can't afford to do this!"

Nadine looked at her. "Yes, I can. I have not even touched most of the material. It was ordered by the Morris boys and delivered. I am just the middleman. Someone has to keep up the paperwork for the government."

Frances said, "Well, if it didn't cost any more than this, I will at least buy some comfortable furniture for the porch for us to rest."

Ron jumped up. "I know where I can unload—I mean, sell you some. It came in last week and is so pretty. It would be great for the porch. If you're interested I can deliver it tomorrow night."

"Good, we can all rest while we make some decisions about how to handle selling the pieces." Frances said as she left to make coffee to have with the pies.

Mark thought it would not be a good idea to have anyone coming out to the church to see the items. Sam felt they should make a selection from several groups and take it to an appraiser. Mark said he would research antique appraisers and make a list for them to look at. Doris Two suggested they take their motor home so everyone could make the trip together. "We can take a few of the pieces of furniture," she added. Then debate started as to when they would be ready. It was finally decided that in two weeks, they would make their first trip.

Everyone started getting ready to leave, and soon, the cars were traveling down the lane. Frances stood at the front of the church, watching the taillights turn toward town and feeling alone. She could hear the sounds of insects and an occasional mockingbird. She looked up through the trees at the sky with all the stars shining and said a prayer, thanking God for the great life he had provided. She could not keep from thinking that it would be better if she had someone to share her happiness with. She was thankful for her friends, but it was not the same as having someone that belonged to you to talk about the day. The cats helped, but there was still something missing.

Chapter 8

The next two weeks were hectic. Contents from the remainder of the hall and several of the side rooms had been moved to the garage. The bed, chest, and Frances's chair had been moved to her room. They had found bolts of fabric in one room, and they used some of that to hang over the windows for temporary privacy. Even with the makeshift curtains, the room was so pleasant. When Frances and the cats fell into bed at night, she had a place that was peaceful. Sleeping in the pretty bed had not helped the cats' behavior. She told them they just could not learn to behave.

On Saturday morning at the end of the first week, everyone was working at a steady pace. Sam, Otis, Mark, and Ron were hauling to the garage, unpacking and calling out to Nadine the item description and marking the control number and the bin number on the item. Each shelf in the garage had been given a bin number, as had areas on the floor of the garage. Frances's car never made it inside her new garage. The tables in the kitchen were also assigned bin numbers. Frances, Doris, Peggy, and Doris Two were taking the small items to the bins assigned as they were processed.

The cats were running wild. Every person taking items to the garage had an escort. When a box was opened, they would stand on their hind legs and peer over the top to see what was inside. Periodically, a cat would jump inside and would have to be rescued. Around noon, all three cats were in the garage sitting on a table, and they turned their heads in the same direction to listen. Hearing what no human ear could hear, they jumped down and ran to the porch. Frances noticed their behavior, but thought it was surely a false alarm. Joseph would have gone back home long ago. She stopped what she was doing and listened. All three cats started their cries simultaneously. There was no mistaking their actions. Doris and Peggy had been peeking out the corner of their eyes and glancing at each other.

Frances turned toward the door to the porch and rubbed the palms of her hands on the side of her shorts. Unconsciously brushing her hair with her fingers, she walked around the rail and up the ramp that Sam and Otis had thought to build to make it easier to move items. She wondered what Joseph wanted this time. Did he want to take the cats back with him? Her mind was racing with numerous alternatives. All three cats were standing tall with their front paws on the screen watching the car. She put down her hand to keep them from following her out the door.

Joseph was getting out of the car with a smile on his face. *Go ahead*, she thought, *Smile that handsome smile. It won't do you any good.* Looking at him with a face she hoped did not show any expression, she said, "Going back to clear your head in the sand again?"

Joseph came up to her, still smiling. "No, I've never left. You always said I attracted work. I hadn't been there two days when I was approached by a businessman about putting together a development for him. I've been working night and day. I had a lot of my office stuff shipped there so I could work. You should see the area. The vegetation is fascinating. He wants as much of the natural beauty left as possible. He believes that if you like a piece of property for the way it is, why come in and destroy it for another cookie-cutter development."

Joseph was looking around while he was talking. Then he hesitated and started in a total new direction of conversation. "What have you done here? This is great. Did you do all this by yourself?" Frances saw him looking at the group of cars outside the garage.

"No, I have lots of help." Frances could not help admiring his tan. His blue eyes reflected the sky as he looked back at her. Neither of them spoke. Frances could not think of a word to say. She could hear the low cries of the cats. It was as if they wanted to be included. Finally, Joseph asked, "May I see your cats?" Frances could only nod as she turned to lead the way to the porch.

As she stepped inside, she was aware of the quiet. The only sound was the purring of the cats. She looked toward the kitchen, and everyone was sitting around the table, not saying a word. In all her conversations with them, she had never mentioned her life before Synaxis and they had never asked. She was sure they were asking themselves millions of questions. She might as well get it over with and make the necessary introductions.

Joseph was suddenly aware of the situation and turned toward the door with her. In her most cheery voice, she said, "Hi, everyone, this is Joseph, my former husband." For a few seconds, no one said a word, then suddenly, they all broke loose. Everyone jumped up at the same time, talking, shaking hands, and smiling. They had Joseph surrounded before he knew what happened. As Joseph looked from one to another, he sneaked a look at Frances and his expression said it all. "Who are these people?" He had never witnessed the chaos of the group when they were in a party mode. They had split after all the handshaking, and Mark and Ron were on the telephone giving a restaurant an order for takeouts, with Sam and Otis standing with them, giving their opinions of what was needed. Mark had broken away from the group to use his cell phone to call the sheriff.

The sheriff had said he'd already seen the car go by. He was loading his tea in the car and had called Mary and Ben. Mary had made cakes and pies that morning. Yes, he would run over to Marshland to pick up the food, he agreed.

Sam and Otis had moved two tables out to the porch and were placing chairs around the tables. Nadine was checking the inventory to locate the bin with the table linens. Frances was taking the china, crystal, and silver out of the china cabinet they had designated for personal use. Joseph had moved up against a wall in the kitchen and was watching the action. The cats were beneath their usual table, peering out at all the movement. They were always careful to keep their tails curled around their bodies. Frances smiled to herself as she looked at Joseph. He looked like someone at a tennis tournament.

Joseph's head turned toward the sound of the siren coming up the lane. His eyebrows went up when Sam said, "Good, here comes the tea." Joseph was caught in the crowd heading to the porch. The men were heading out to help with the food. When Mary and Ben came in, the chaos went around the room again with introductions. In no time, the food was on the table and everyone was in their seat. Joseph looked over and all three cats were in a corner with crystal dishes containing fresh food.

After lunch, Sam and Otis had Joseph by the arm and were giving him a tour of their garage. Frances thought of it as *their* garage since it would not have been possible without them. Being an architect, Joseph could not believe the construction of the addition. They explained they wanted to keep the same lines of the church so as to not destroy the elements. When Joseph asked the name of the architect, they just grinned. When he asked about the blueprints, they just touched their heads with their finger.

Next, they took him down the hall, showing him the bedroom and how they had moved the doors to different locations and not used any new materials, just recycling what was already in the room. They opened doors to the rooms that had been cleared and shelves installed to hold the items ready for appraisal. They opened doors to show him what it looked like before everyone started. When they entered the sanctuary, at first, Joseph was overwhelmed by all the items in the room. As he started walking around looking at the walls, ceiling, and windows, he was speechless. He could not believe that anyone would let a piece of property just sit and not be used for so many years. Sam and Otis would uncover a piece of furniture ever so often and all three men would run their hands over the finish, admiring what someone had created. Sam and Otis had come back to the porch, and when Frances went to check on Joseph, he was standing with his hands in his pockets, looking at one of the windows. As she stood in the door watching him, he lowered his head for a few minutes and looked up at the window again. He must have sensed her standing at the door for he turned around and smiled at her. "You really have found a jewel."

When they went back to the kitchen, all the work had continued. Joseph followed Frances to the garage and started helping them return the items to the proper place after it had been inventoried and put the box on the stack that was almost as high as the ceiling. "What are you going to do when you run out of room for the boxes?" Joseph asked.

Everyone hesitated a minute, and Frances finally said, "I guess we had not taken the time to resolve that problem."

"What is in the buildings at the edge of the yard near the woods?" Joseph asked Otis. Sam and Otis looked at each other and one of them said, "We never looked." The silence was one that Frances knew well by this time. She could not wait for Joseph's reaction to this ritual.

Just then, Ron and Mark came into the garage carrying a small desk. They could tell by the atmosphere something was happening. "What?" Mark asked. Everyone stopped what they were doing and they all headed for the door. Sam and Otis led the way. Joseph looked at Frances and she tilted her head with a silly smile and said, "Well, come on!"

They had headed first to the largest of the buildings. As they stood outside the barn, they looked at the padlock that blocked their way. Nadine said, "Padlocks are cheap. All we need to do is cut it off." Sam told Ron he had some bolt cutters in his tool box and he took off to get them. They were soon removing the lock and opening the doors to let in the sunlight.

They lined up across the opening of the barn and stared inside. Finally, Otis said, "Just what I suspected." Everyone was still quiet.

Joseph asked, "What is it?"

Everyone said together, "More crates."

They slowly went in different directions, walking among the crates and looking in stalls. Someone climbed the ladder to inspect the contents of the loft. Mark said, "It's the same as the house."

Frances told Joseph, "It's going to take me years to process all this."

Joseph laughed. "At least you won't be unemployed."

The next building was not as full. Evidently, it had been the last one used to store materials and whoever had started the collection quit before it was completely full. Frances said maybe they could move some if the items to that building to make it easier to organize.

The last building was completely empty. Now they could store the boxes. Sam and Otis reported that the roofs were in good condition, and even though the floors were dirt, everything had been placed on boards and appeared to be dry. None of the items they had checked seemed to be damaged.

Everyone went back to the porch to discuss the strategy for the next week. James said he was going to take any unnecessary items out of the motor home to make room for the inventory for appraisal. He had checked, and there was enough room for everyone to sit while riding. "It'll be a little tight, but we can make it." Frances had looked at Joseph when mention was made of the trip and she saw he looked disappointed that he was not going.

Sam said they could leave early on Monday morning and could be in Atlanta for lunch. Everyone was dividing the tasks to be done during the trip. James told Joseph, "You have to be good with figures since you're an architect, so your job will be to help Nadine with the laptop." Frances saw his eyes light up when he found out he was going to be included. How on earth was she going to deal with this situation? Oh well, she would worry when and if the time came.

The sheriff said he would stay in town to watch out for everything. James could let everyone know that if they needed medicine they could call the drugstore in Marshland and the sheriff would pick it up and they could come to the station. Mary said she would pick up all the calls and take messages. Ron said if Frances didn't care, he would come out to the church to sleep. He realized it had been there for years without anyone bothering anything, but there was no need to take a chance. Frances was relieved, knowing she would not have to worry about the cats.

Chapter 9

To say the next week was hectic would be an understatement. Frances and all her friends worked from early morning until late at night. When she would fall into bed at night, the cats appeared to be just as exhausted. They had taken just about every step that everyone else had. They did not make a noise or have any spats over territory on the bed. They just flopped wherever they could get.

Joseph had driven over from the coast on Saturday and Sunday to help. A year ago, he would not have taken time from his work to help her with a project. He was there for breakfast and stayed for dessert at night. No one asked any questions or made any comments. They just acted as if this were normal.

On the morning of the *big trip*, Frances heard a car coming up the lane. She lifted her head to look at the clock and noted it was six-thirty. She did not need to look out the window to see who was coming. All three cats shot off the bed and headed to the kitchen and started their "He's here" cries. Frances got up and put on a robe to go unlock the door. Joseph came in carrying large bakery boxes. "I thought we could use some snacks."

She made her usual working pot of coffee and went back to get dressed. She could hear Joseph talking to the cats. They had managed to convince him they had not had treats in days, and it might be days before they would eat again. She looked in the mirror at herself and thought about all the times they had sat talking to the cats and caring for them. When she was finished, she went back to the kitchen and found Joseph sitting in a chair with Zeus in his lap.

The cats' ears went up and they raised their heads. Frances and Joseph could not hear anything but knew something was happening. In a few minutes, they heard the engines as the vehicles came up the drive. The sheriff was leading the motor home with his lights flashing. The motor home pulled up in front of the garage and Mark and Ron opened the garage doors.

Everyone grabbed their coffee cup, poured a fast refill, and carried it out with them to work. There was no sitting on the porch. Peggy looked inside the bakery boxes with an "Oh my!" and took them out to the motor home for the trip. All three cats were sitting on the porch watching the loading. They were not making a sound. Frances looked at them and thought they had the same expression as Joseph when he thought he was not going to get to go.

In a record hour, everything was loaded and secured. Sam and the sheriff had gone inside to check everything before they left. In a few minutes, they came out with Sam carrying one of the carriers and the sheriff the other two. "What are you doing?" asked Frances, puzzled. Everyone said, "We can't go without the babies." You could almost see the smiles on the cat's faces. They were placed on a ledge over the driver's and passenger's seats. There were windows all around and they could see out. Doris Two said the space could be used for extra sleeping area, but they thought it would be a good place for the cats to ride. Frances was so happy they accepted her pets. She dreaded having to leave them. They had never been away from her.

The sheriff had given them an escort to the city limits. He loved using those lights. Frances realized that she had never been beyond the stores in town since she arrived. She looked out the windows at the homes they were passing. The people who were already outside waved as they went by. The sheriff would sound the siren and James would blow the horn.

Frances noticed how the shuffling for seats had been arranged and the little footwork in making sure Joseph was sitting next to her. She thought, *You sly dogs. You are trying to play matchmaker.* Joseph did not seem to notice or didn't mind. She wished she could figure out what he was up to. He obviously was enjoying her new friends. He had never had the relaxed attitude he was exhibiting. He had reached over and wiped her chin when powdered sugar had dropped off the roll. As he brushed, he was looking into her eyes. She saw Doris punch Nadine in the ribs.

They had spent one evening while they were resting to decide the best appraisers to approach. They had decided to go to several and compare what each had to say. Ron had been in charge of the maps and had moved to the passenger seat to give James directions to their first stop. They had made excellent time and decided they would make one stop before lunch. Parking the vehicle was going to be a major problem. Frances and Nadine got off in front of the first stop. Frances's heart was pounding, and she was terrified that she would say the wrong thing. She wanted to get the best price for the items for she had spent many nights thinking of the things she could do with the money. She did not want for herself. All she wanted was peace and contentment. Her first order of business after everything had been handled was the cemetery. Next, she wanted to get computers for the schools. A new piano for the church in town was also on her list.

The first proprietor was a man. Frances did not like the fact that she made snap judgments about people, but she was usually (although not in Doris's case) right. The man approached them with an air of stuffiness as he peered down his nose at them.

Frances extended her hand and introduced herself. He looked down at her hand, and she thought at first glance he was not going to shake it. She explained to him they had some pieces they would like for him to examine. He informed them he normally made his inspections on site and he would check his appointment book to see when he was available to make this visit.

"How about right now?" Nadine questioned.

He adjusted his glasses and looked at her. "Now?"

He had looked at their empty hands. "Yes, they are outside."

He again adjusted his glasses again. "Outside?"

Frances said, "They are circling the block."

He appeared to turn pale. Glancing over his shoulder at his assistant who was standing nearby, he repeated, "Circling the block?"

Good grief, thought Frances. *Is this man daffy.*

He stood in place a few minutes without saying a word. He finally said, "Perhaps I have a few minutes."

The trio went out to the sidewalk and saw the motor home coming around the corner. When they pulled up to the curb, Mark opened the side door and stepped out to let them board. Sam was standing inside and gestured for the appraiser to go up front and be seated at the table. James pulled back out in traffic, and the appraiser looked as if he was going to faint. Frances suddenly thought, *He probably thinks he is being abducted by a band of burglars*. She could not resist smiling. About that time, he looked up and saw the three cats peering down at him from their carriers. He placed his hand over his heart again. "Cats!"

"Don't worry," Otis told him. "We know what they're worth."

A pad was placed on the table to protect the items and Joseph placed the first piece in front of the appraiser. Frances and Peggy were watching the appraiser's face closely to see what reaction he would have. Peggy gave her a gentle nudge that would not be noticed by anyone else. He cleared his throat and turned the piece gently around for inspection. He told them of the good quality, condition, and gave what Frances thought was a high appraisal.

Nadine was busy at her laptop and had entered the information into her database.

Frances glanced out the window as Mark was handing the appraiser the next piece. She saw they were passing the front of the appraiser's business and his assistant was standing our front talking on a telephone. He had one hand up in the air and was obviously unsure of his employer's condition. *What if he is calling the police? This is not Synaxis.* She could just imagine being surrounded by a SWAT team and ordered out of the vehicle with their hands up.

The appraiser was again apparently pleased. He gave them another favorable value. While the piece was being removed, he took out his handkerchief and dabbed at his palms. Frances wondered if it was from fright or excitement of seeing the pieces. When the third piece was placed on the table, he uttered, "This is incredible. May I ask where you obtained the pieces?" He looked from one to the other, since he could not decide who the owner was.

Frances did not want to give too much information, but did not want him to think they were thieves. "I purchased an estate and these are some of the items that went with the property. I'm interested in disposing of a few pieces to help me restore the property."

The appraiser was obviously interested and said he would be glad to make an offer on some of the items for his personal collection. He directed James to drive a couple of blocks to a parking lot where the motor home could be parked.

Everyone was becoming more relaxed, and the appraiser had gone to the back of the motor home to see the pieces of furniture they had brought. Frances watched him touch the pieces, examining every detail. He asked how to contact her in the future, and she gave him the e-mail address that had been set up. He then asked if she had a reference. She went against her better judgment, but gave him Mr. Whitehead as a reference. When he was finished, he shook hands with everyone and even spoke to each cat in turn.

The assistant was obviously relieved when the appraiser stepped out of the motor home. They looked back and could see the expression on the appraiser's face as he was talking to his assistant. The assistant would put his hand to his mouth and you could almost hear him say, "Really?"

The group discussed the appraiser's good points, bad points, and credentials. Would they use him again? Would they trust him to come to Synaxis to see the entire collection? They had a lot of decisions to make. As Frances leaned back in the seat, she was glad she had them to help her. She would never have been this far along if she had struck out on her own. She would still be trying to scratch out a place in the kitchen, and it would have been months before she could have found someone to do appraisals. How on earth would she have managed?

They were looking out the windows for a place to pick up lunch, having decided they would eat in the motor home at lunch to save time. They saw a small restaurant and James pulled over to the curb. Joseph and Mark went in to place the orders. When they came out, Ron went out to help them. The boxes were piled high. It was a good thing everyone was working so hard. They would gain weight if they were not.

As the food was being assembled, Joseph took one of the boxes and opened it to show baked chicken. Three servings were placed in the carriers for the cats.

They were able to see two other appraisers that afternoon. Both had given the same positive values as the first. The group had selected one other appraiser, and they decided they would see him the next day before heading back home. Mark had reserved rooms at a motel that had parking for the motor home. Doris and Frances were going to share a room, and Joseph asked if he could keep the cats with him for the night. Frances told him that the three would probably enjoy his company.

After they had checked in and cleaned up, they decided to eat in the restaurant across the street. The cats were left in the room with a "Do not disturb" sign on the door.

That night after the lights were turned out, Doris asked, "Do you want to talk about it?"

Frances thought for a minute. "I really don't know what to say. I guess we just went through a period where we only had the cats in common. Joseph was wrapped up in his work. I tried to make our home perfect. We just quit talking."

After another silence, Doris asked, "Do you still love him?"

Frances paused. "Now that I stop to think about loving him, I guess I never really stopped. Love is something that is always inside you, you just choose to think about it or hide your feelings from yourself."

That seemed to satisfy Doris and she did not ask any more questions.

The next morning, they saw the last appraiser, who also gave favorable values to the items. Then they headed back home. It had been a productive trip. They would decide which one could be easily used in the future.

Frances was tired when they got back home and was glad everyone was going home after everything was unloaded and put in its proper place. They all agreed to rest the next day.

Joseph was the last to leave. As he was standing on the porch telling the cats good-bye, he looked at Frances. "Have you been to the coast?" She shook her head no.

"It's only a twenty-minute drive and you would enjoy the place. Why don't you come over next Sunday and bring the cats?"

She thought for a few moments, then agreed, "All right."

"I'll call you with the directions," he said as he went out the door. She realized he could have given them to her then, but thought he probably wanted an excuse to call her during the week.

That evening, she was relaxing with the cats on the porch when the telephone rang. When she answered, she heard Mr. Whitehead's voice: "Well, Frances, how are you?"

Frances held the receiver away from her ear for a moment. "I'm fine, Mr. Whitehead. I am surprised to hear from you."

"I've had time to think about the telephone call and I just can't think of you living in the conditions you described, so I've decided I will relieve you of the property and give you your money back." He was talking to her as if he really believed what he was saying.

"Oh, don't worry, Mr. Whitehead. I have adjusted. I've spent a lot of time working on the place and have developed a home-like feeling."

After a minute, he said, "I would never think of you doing all that work for nothing. I could give you $25,000 for your work… if you let me buy the place back from you."

Frances leaned her head back against the lounge and tried to keep from laughing into the receiver. "That's all right, Mr. Whitehead, a deal is a deal, and I don't want to uproot the cats again. I appreciate your offer. Thanks for calling."

She immediately hung up the receiver. She then called James and told him about the conversation. He said he wished he had been there to see Whitehead's face. They talked about the appraiser they were nearly certain must have called Whitehead and told him what she was trying to sell. "That confirms our original opinion—we don't trust him. There's no way I would let him near this place. I know it sounds crazy, but I think I should have an alarm system installed. The sheriff is good, but they could come in from another direction."

Frances called Nadine next and told her what had happened and that she wanted to install an alarm system. She got the name of the company in Marshland that Ron and Mark used and made a note to call them first thing in the morning.

That night, she did not sleep well, having one crazy nightmare after another. The cats kept moving around, sensing her emotions.

She finally got up before dawn and sat on the porch with her coffee to watch the sunrise. She had forgotten how much she enjoyed that time of the morning.

As soon as she thought the security company was open, she called and made an appointment. They may be able to start that afternoon if the crew finished their current job.

She wandered around inside, looking in all the rooms and finally ended up in the sanctuary. She sat down on a pew and stared at one of the windows. She thought about what she would say if Joseph decided to ask her to let him come back. She knew she had said she would worry about it when the time came, but she needed to sort out her feelings now. She must not let her being lonely affect her decision.

She heard a car coming up the drive. It was too soon for the installers to be coming. She went down the hall to the kitchen as the four women were getting out of the car. "I thought you were going to rest today," she said in greeting.

"We didn't say we couldn't sit and talk," Doris said, and they all nodded in agreement.

"Have you looked up?" Nadine asked. Frances knew before she got next to them what was going on. Sitting on the ledge of the belfry were all three cats. She had ceased to worry about them, so they went inside to the porch.

They all agreed that she was right to have a security system installed. Frances said she was trying to decide if they would think she was totally crazy if she put a system on the barn as well. Peggy laughed. "You would have something no one else in Synaxis has, a burglar-proof barn."

Doris commented, "I can't think of anyone in the south that has a burglar-proof barn."

Looking around, Frances said, "Well, we'll soon find out. Here comes the truck."

As the security company truck pulled up in front of the garage, two men got out and were looking up. The driver came up to the porch and asked, "Do you know you have cats in your belfry?" Everyone laughed.

Everyone went inside to show the installers the church first. The men looked at the kitchen and eyed each other at all the tables with boxes sitting on top and beneath them. As they went down the hall, they stopped in the bedroom first. Both of the men walked over to the bed and gave it a good going over. The second man said he had never seen anything like that in his life.

By the time they got to the sanctuary, they stopped dead still. Frances could not help saying, "I haven't finished unpacking yet."

The men worked their way around the room trying to figure the best way to install the wiring and where to put the control panel. Frances told them it would need to be put in the kitchen. When they asked where the electrical panel was located, all the women looked at each other. Nadine said, "They had to have used it when they connected the wiring for the computer and clothes dryer. Uh, oh, the basement."

One of the installers said, "I don't like the way you said that."

Peggy led the way through the labyrinth to the door to the basement. As they went down the stairs, pulling on the lights, the men were becoming more curious. When they saw the crates, they shrugged, and one of them said, "More unpacking to do, I presume."

When the women had settled on the porch, they giggled for fifteen minutes about the expressions of the two men when they saw all the packing boxes and crates. Doris said, "By the time they went through the house, they didn't think it was unusual for you to have cats in your belfry."

Nadine commented, "Wait until they see the barn."

One of the installers came out on the porch. "We hate to ask you, but could you get your cats? They're playing with the wires and we're afraid they'll get hurt—to say nothing of slowing down our progress."

Frances apologized as she went to the door and called them. They immediately came trotting down the hall, and she closed the door behind them. Not liking the fact they were blocked from their new game, they proceeded to cry and paw at the door from a while.

"Get over it," Frances told them.

The women discussed not doing any unpacking while any workmen were around. They all felt it would be better to have as few people as possible knowing what was located at the church. They had plenty to do with paperwork and searching for buyers for the items they planned to sell first.

Frances told them they needed to help her pick out a lamp to give J. T.'s wife. That was all the payment he had wanted. They should deliver it as soon as the workmen left. She had some more work she needed to get J. T. to start. She would insist on paying him for any additional work he did. She had decided she could not wait until the first sale to start working on the cemetery. There was really no need to wait to start work; she could always use some of her money. Her fear of not having money to live on had stopped. Her expenses were less than she had budgeted.

She needed to get a business account opened to handle the paperwork for what she spent and the income from the collection. She also needed to get additional insurance on the contents. She had totally forgotten about insurance. There were so many decisions she had to make. And she had thought her new life was going to be simple.

That evening, after everyone had left, the telephone rang, and when Frances answered, she heard the voice of her friend from back home. "Anne! I've really missed you. How have you been?"

"I'm fine. I thought I would have heard from you, but I finally tracked you down. Have you heard the gossip?"

Frances thought for a minute. "No, I have not had any contact with my friends. I've been so busy trying to settle into my new home. There's a lot more work than I anticipated. What is going on?"

"Well, Joseph suddenly called his office one day a couple of weeks ago and said he needed to get some rest. Everyone expected him to be gone a day or two—you know how he is about work. Anyway, he has not returned to work. He hasn't been home and his secretary said he had sent for some of his things from the office. He told her he had a little job to do. She said he gave her an address on the coast of Georgia. When I looked it up on the map, I noticed it isn't far from where you're living."

Frances smiled. "Between you and me, I have seen him. He came by here on his way over to the coast and asked to see the cats. He really missed them. I think he would have preferred to give me everything and take the cats."

Anne could not believe her ears. "You let him see the cats? I cannot imagine what is going through your head. He made you miserable, and now, you act like nothing is wrong. Are your sure you are not sick?"

Frances assured her, "I'm fine. I don't think I've had this much peace of mind in a long time. You cannot believe the effect this place has had on me. In spite of the condition, it has made me stop and examine my life and what I really want. At first, I was shocked and thought I'd made a mistake, but within twenty-four hours, I came to realize this is where I was meant to be. I will be starting a project tomorrow that I feel I owe to the property."

Anne laughed. "It sounds like the place is alive. You don't even sound like the same person. I think I'm going to have to come see for myself."

"Come on down. I could use another set of hands. Bring your work clothes and don't expect to get a lot of rest. You will have to let me know if you're coming. I will need to clean out a room and get a bed for you to sleep in. I only have one bed, and you know after the three cats take up their space, there isn't a lot of room left. I only have one bath and it's primitive by your standards."

"Now you have me curious. Are you sure you're not leading me along just to get me to come see you?"

"Cross my heart," Frances said, making an X over her heart.

"Let me check my schedule and see what I can work out. I think I need some of that medicine," Anne replied.

After they hung up, Frances wondered why she didn't tell Anne about her trip to Atlanta. They had always shared everything with each other. It was as if she were afraid to say anything for fear of jinxing what may happen. Anne was the first person with whom she was able to share her thoughts and feelings without fear of being ridiculed. "No," she told the cats, "this is something better shared in person. I think it needs the atmosphere of this place to really put it in perspective."

The telephone rang again and Frances answered. This time, she heard Joseph's voice: "Are you busy?"

Frances smiled and said, "No, I just got off the phone with Anne. You should hear the gossip about you."

Joseph said he figured that was who it was. "Mary had said it was a proper sounding lady and told me where the call was coming from and I told her that was a friend of yours. She called me back when you hung up. I can't believe the telephone service there. It's like stepping back in time. I wanted to ask her what you were saying, but did not want to spoil her fun."

Frances told him about their conversation. He shared with her how his project was going and asked how work was progressing with her. They laughed so hard when she told him about the security installers. She told him they were coming back tomorrow to finish the house and then she was going to tell them about the barn. He said he wished he could be there to watch.

The cats evidently could sense who was on the phone because they were standing up and rubbing against her. Frances had to take the cord out of Zeus's mouth several times to keep him from biting it. Star finally crawled up in her lap to sleep. Sunshine was content to just lay and watch. When she finally hung up the phone, she looked at the clock, she realized they had been talking for over an hour. "That's a first," she said out loud.

Chapter 10

The next morning, the area in front of the garage was full of vehicles. The installers arrived last. Everyone was on the porch having their breakfast when they came. Otis told them to come on in and have coffee with them before they started, and if they were hungry, there was plenty of food. Doris had been bringing groceries and everyone was chipping in and eating well and not spending very much money. Ron told her if she was going to continue to run a halfway house for people looking for excitement, she was going to have to get a decent kitchen. They had become accustomed to juggling stove eyes to make them work.

After everyone had finished, Sam stood up and told the installers he would go with them to the barn to unlock the door. Everyone watched as the installers looked at each other and finally asked, "Why do you need to unlock the barn?"

"So you can install a security system," Sam said without a blink. You would think this was something he did every day. The men strapped on their tool belts, and off they went. After they left, Otis said that he was going to the barn also, that he and Sam had decided to stay out with them. It would give them time to walk around and work out a plan in their heads. They thought they would install a hoist to get the boxes out of the loft. "We're going to have to run electricity out to the barn. We called to have the lines put in. They should be here today."

Frances exclaimed, "I can't believe you two. You think of everything. If we didn't have our agreement, I could never have afforded all the help you've given me."

Everyone seemed pleased with their arrangement. Each week, everyone had made a selection from the inventory. They told Frances they would never be able to find anything to compare with what they were getting. Frances loved seeing their faces when they made their selections. She was so glad she could share with them her great fortune of having found this place.

That afternoon, the lines were run for electricity to the barn and the security system was completed. Frances was sure there would be a lot of speculation in Marshland about what was going on in Synaxis. Otis had said he heard one of the installers say, "That woman sure has a lot of unpacking to do. I wonder what her house looked like where she lived before."

Sam and Otis said they had figured a way to improve storage in the barn and probably move some of the items out of the sanctuary to make it easier to work. They could take the tables out of the garage to the barn. "We could sort and inventory there and not have to move anything up to the house."

Frances told the group she thought they should buy equipment to help with the work. They also needed to get a phone installed at the barn.

They had found an international auction house about a day away and thought it would be a good idea to check them out. They could rent a truck to transport the items. Nadine sent an e-mail to them and made an appointment for two weeks later to take a load and see how it moved. They would have the items available for inspection for a month and would catalog them for their sale the following month.

That evening, when Joseph called, Frances told him of their plans. He said he would like to go with them if she didn't mind. She was glad he brought up the subject because she was shy about asking him. He told her he was e-mailing the directions for her to come over on Sunday. They talked about friends they'd back home, how the cats were doing, his progress at the coast, how long it would take him to finish, what she would like to do to her property, his ideas on improving the property, and finally said good night.

J. T. and his sons started work on the cemetery the next day. When everyone found out what she was doing, they were so pleased. Sam said it was a shame what had been allowed to happen. No one had been out here in years. People had forgotten about the church and did not even remember there was a cemetery. It was decided that when enough of the growth had been removed, they would take off a day to work on cleaning the markers. Nadine told them she had some solutions that would probably do the job. She would order more brushes and buckets. Peggy said she had the rubber gloves in her shop.

On the second day, the group, armed with their tools, walked to the cemetery to start work. Frances noticed they all worked close to each other rather than spreading out. They started at the edge where she had first entered the cemetery. She could not believe the transformation. All the weeds were gone and the azaleas had been trimmed. J. T. explained the azaleas would not be pretty for a while. They would fill back out after they had adjusted to the pruning. They would not have many blooms next year since they had been trimmed the wrong time of the year. He would come out next year after they bloomed, trim and feed them, and they would be back to normal the following year.

No one was talking. You could hear the sound of the brushes on the stones.

It had been a long time since Frances had felt so good about a job. She felt she was finally giving something rather than taking.

She had never known the people beneath the stones, but she could feel their spirits and know they had probably loved the church, and it had been an important part of their lives. She wondered why the church had been abandoned. Its beauty was a testimony of those in the community who had come here. She could almost visualize the people coming to the church and cemetery.

Doris said in a low voice, "Peggy, you and Nadine come here a minute." When they were beside her, she said, "This is our great-grandparents. I did not know they were here." All three women stood silently looking down. Frances stood up and walked over to them. Sam and Otis took off their caps and joined the group.

"I never knew this is where they were," Doris said in a shaky voice. "My mother rarely mentioned them. I have neglected this place when I should have found out who was here and had enough respect for my heritage to help take care of the grounds." They each turned around and looked at the other stones. "There are probably ancestors of others living in Synaxis buried here. Frances, would you mind if people came out here to look?"

Frances shook her head. The moment seemed so solemn she could not speak. She could never deny anyone access to this place. She thought it was her destiny to come here and make friends with these people who could help her renew the town with its past.

J. T. and the sons saw them standing and thought something was wrong. They put down their tools and came over to check. "Is everything all right?" Otis explained to them what they discovered, and J. T. said he would help them with the scrubbing as soon as he was finished with the weeds and shrubs.

They all went back to work and forgot about the time. They had not stopped for lunch, and they heard voices coming from the edge of the cemetery. "Are you still here?"

Recognizing Ron's voice, Peggy asked, "Why are you home so early?"

Ron and Mark looked at each other. "It is six o'clock," Mark said.

It had become a ritual that everyone gathered at the church for dinner at night. James was setting the table when the work crew marched up the lane to the porch. "I wish you could see yourselves," he told them. They stopped to inspect each other and decided they better divide themselves between the kitchen and the bathroom to wash their faces and hands. The cats were milling around their feet, sniffing at them and trying to figure out where they had been.

They filled in James, Mark, and Ron regarding the stones at the cemetery. Each one said they probably had ancestors buried there. James suggested a listing of the information on the stones be prepared and distributed to the people in the community. "We can have copies at various locations for people to pick up." Frances thought that was a great idea. "We need to take one day a week for working on the cemetery. Maybe some of the other people would like to help."

That night, when Joseph called Frances, she was already dozing in her chair. One cat was asleep in her lap and the other two at her feet. When she answered, he asked, "Did I wake you?"

She told him about their day in the cemetery and their ideas about it. He thought it was a great idea. He said he would even volunteer some time to the project. Frances could not believe this was Joseph. He would never have done anything like this before. She did not know what kind of sand he had used at the beach to clear his head, but it would sell to wives all over America if she could find out. He asked her if she understood his directions for Sunday and reminded her not to forget the cats.

Later, Frances lay in the huge bathtub with warm water and soaked the kinks out of her body. The cats lay on the floor beside the tub and washed, taking turns helping each other with parts that were not easy to reach. Sunshine must have gotten too rough with one of Star's ears and she decided that was enough and a hissing party started up. Frances, not even opening her eyes, told them to shut up.

Chapter 11

The next day, work resumed on getting pieces ready to take to the auction. Lights had been installed in the barn and shelving had been put in the stalls for storing and grouping of small pieces. Everyone hauled the boxes out of the stalls and the tables had been brought from the house. They decided to break for lunch before starting the unpacking and sorting.

Frances thought more and more of the good she could do with the proceeds from the sale of the articles. As she uncovered the items, she could not believe the value. She had to respect the desire of the community not to be overtaken by outsiders wanting to exploit the environment or residence by forcing changes they did not want. Now that she understood their desire to keep their homes peaceful, she wanted the same. Her desire to use part of the earnings for her projects was another reason she had to work out her feelings for Joseph before things went too far. Joseph would think she was crazy. Still, she felt this property had been preserved for someone that would use it for good. It was ironic that a church had been selected to preserve the property of the estate.

When Frances brought up the subject of helping the community with some of the proceeds, everyone was speechless. She quickly explained that she had developed the same respect for community values and would never jeopardize their ideals. When they realized she did indeed understand, they were all smiles. Their determination for progress for the sale was doubled. No matter how tired anyone became, they kept up the pace.

Joseph came over the middle of the week and brought dinner. He had called ahead and told them he was "cooking" that night. When they heard his car drive up to the porch, they started finishing the task they were working on and checked the building before turning on the security system.

When the group entered the porch, the cats were following Joseph around the table as he put out the food. They divided in their two groups and went to the two sinks to wash their hands. As they started eating, they decided Joseph was a good cook.

Everyone was so tired, they decided they would quit work early that evening. Frances approached them with an idea she had to preserve the antiques and still make money. She said she would have enough money from the first auction to keep her going for another couple of years, if she managed well. She did not have a lot of material needs—just the serenity of the church, friends, and her cats. She had decided she might write a book. If her luck continued, it might make her enough money to keep her alive. She wanted the antiques to be enjoyed by everyone and not just a select few that could afford to purchase them. She wondered if she could find a suitable house in a nearby town that could be used as a museum. The antiques could be displayed and people could pay a modest price to tour the home. Perhaps, in time, the museum could be used for teas, receptions, etc.

While she was talking, she noticed Joseph's expression when she said she did not need a lot of money. His eyes had lowered and she could detect a slight frown on his face. She hoped no one else noticed. She quickly looked around and everyone was looking at her.

James said he thought that was a great idea. "You'd be surprised what a great demand there is for places like you just described. I'm sure it would be well received. Everyone else gave similar responses.

Joseph asked, "Does anyone know who owns the estate between Synaxis and Marshland? It's about halfway and appears to be vacant. The house sits well off the highway and there are large trees."

Doris thought for a minute. "Yes, I'd forgotten all about that place. The lady who owns the property broke her hip and has been in an assisted living home until she's able to return. She's a wonderful person. Why don't we visit her and see what she has to say. I am afraid she'll never be able to return to her home and I don't think she has any close family."

Joseph looked at Frances and asked, "Can't several of us go see her tomorrow and let her know our plans?"

Frances replied, "You never know the answer until you ask the question. Why not!"

Chapter 12

After everyone had left, Frances locked all the doors, checked the windows, and fell into bed. The cats had already stretched out on the bed and she had to declare her territory. She was asleep before the cats were even settled.

Frances was awake before she was aware of what was going on. She did not know if it was the cats or the noise that woke her. The cats had run from the room, as if afraid for their lives. Frances had jumped up, half asleep, and was running behind them. When she got to the kitchen, she was aware that she was standing in the middle of the floor and the noise was still going on. Zeus had jumped up in the window and was looking out. Frances became aware that the loud noise was coming from the barn. It was a loud siren or horn. "The burglar alarm!" she said aloud.

Hurriedly, she put on her shoes and grabbed her keys. Being careful to close the door, she ran as fast as she could toward the barn. The closer she got, the louder the alarm. When she got to the door, she was working frantically trying to get the right key into the lock. Mad at herself for not bringing a flashlight, she finally opened the door and turned on the light. Punching numbers, she finally silenced the noise. Leaning against the wall, she let out a sigh. Then she heard another siren. "Is that the alarm at the house?" she asked herself.

Running back toward the house, she saw the flashing red lights of the sheriff's car coming up the lane. *That's his siren. I guess I've made his day—he loves to use it*, she thought.

The car pulled up beside her and he got out. "What happened?"

Frances was suddenly aware that she was standing there in the dark in her gown. Thankful he didn't even seem to notice, she replied, "I don't know. The alarm came on and I had to get the door open to turn it off. I'm sorry it took me so long. I'll have the security firm check it in the morning. There must have been a malfunction."

He stood looking at the barn for a few minutes, then told her, without even looking at her, to go back to the house, he would lock up.

Frances went back and found a robe to put on, then walked out onto the porch. The sheriff had pulled the car up near the barn and had a search light turned, illuminating the barn. He was walking around with a flashlight, shining it up and down the sides of the building. Then Frances heard another car coming up the lane. Mark and Ron came around the drive, and when they saw the lights at the barn, they drove on up the path without stopping. The three men walked around together as the sheriff continued to shine his light up the sides of the barn. They talked for what seemed like an eternity to Frances. They finally walked toward the woods, looking at the ground. After a few minutes, they returned to the barn, evidently resetting the alarm and locking the door.

Ron and Mark gave her a little wave as they went past the garage. The sheriff pulled up and told her, "No problem. It was probably just an animal that set it off. You go on back to bed and don't worry."

Frances thanked him, went inside, locked the doors, and turned out the lights. She looked at the clock beside the bed and saw it was 4:00 a.m. She leaned over to turn off the lamp and the cats, with the exception of Sunshine, were sitting on the bed, still looking frightened. She gave them a rub to calm them and told them to go to sleep. Looking around for Sunshine, she saw his tail sticking out from behind the drapes. He was sitting in the window. She got out of bed in the dark and went over to the window to get Sunshine. When she pulled the drape back, she looked outside. Sunshine was looking toward the woods where the lane comes out of the cemetery. Sitting at the edge was the sheriff's car, lights out. "Sure, nothing to worry about. I have an armed guard to take care of me. I would have told him he could sleep on the porch."

The sound of the Morris boys' truck woke her early next morning. She felt as if she had run a marathon. After staggering to the kitchen to make coffee, she walked onto the porch and saw that the sheriff had come out of his hiding place and the three men were talking outside the barn. It was basically the same scenario as previously—walking around the barn and looking up.

While the coffee was making, she went to take her bath. If she was to meet everyone at nine o'clock, she would have to hurry. The cats sat beside the tub while she bathed and did their morning wash. She talked to them as if they understood what she was saying. They looked at her as if to say, "Yeah, yeah, be good. You're going off. You'll be back. We won't worry."

The three women were waiting for her when she got to town. Frances saw them stop talking and look at each other when she pulled up. They all seemed too animated. They were always bubbly, but today, they were over the edge. Frances could not believe visiting an elderly woman in a home would wind them up this tight. Peggy spoke first. "I gave Joseph directions and he's going to meet us in Marshland." Then they all piled into Nadine's car and off they went.

Joseph was waiting outside when they arrived. Frances was so nervous she could barely speak. He gave her a reassuring smile and joined the group as they went inside. Doris made inquiries at the desk, and they were directed to a bright porch where residents were lined up in wheelchairs and rockers. The lady who was helping them went over to pretty lady with white hair sitting in a wheelchair. "Mrs. Stubblefield, you have company. These nice people live in Synaxis, and they would like to visit with you."

She smiled up at them and appeared to be sincerely glad to see them. It didn't seem she cared that she didn't know. Doris made the introductions, and they were taken to a small private area where they could all sit. Doris reminded the lady that she had visited her home when she was young. Mrs. Stubblefield remembered them and had a little story to tell them about their parents. Frances stared around the group and could see the pleasure they had remembering. One thing about changing your life, you don't have people around you to remind you of the good times. On the other hand, no one could remind you about the bad times either.

Mrs. Stubblefield finally looked at them and said, "It is wonderful to have you visit, but I feel you have a mission."

Frances leaned forward in her chair. "Mrs. Stubblefield, I mentioned to my friends last night that I would like to have a place to share my antiques with others, perhaps a beautiful house, where people could visit and enjoy them. Not have them locked up and enjoyed by a few. Joseph mentioned your home and how pretty it was. I was wondering if you would consider selling or renting. I realize when you are better, you will want to return, and I'm sure we can work out a plan that would be pleasing to you."

Mrs. Stubblefield sat straighter in her chair. She was quiet for a minute. Frances dreaded hearing her say no. She finally started speaking in a low voice, "I have been very worried since my accident. My home was so important to me. It was a burden and I wished at times I was free, but I did not know what to do. I didn't want just anyone in my house. I had lived there for eighty years. After I was moved to the Assisted Living Residence for therapy,

I found I had been missing the friendship and companionship of those around me. I would go for days without even talking with anyone when I was alone. I don't want to go back to that life. You have answered a prayer for me. I will do anything to help you. I know you'll not do anything to make me ashamed of giving up my home. I will have my attorney contact you with arrangements. I only want to see it when you are finished."

Frances could not stop the tears that came running down her cheeks. Joseph fished out a white handkerchief and handed it to her. "She always cries when she's happy," he said. There were hugs all around, and Peggy went to see if she could get a pitcher of tea to celebrate. Mrs. Stubblefield asked Nadine if she would go to the manager's office and tell her that she would like to have the key to her house brought to her.

Mrs. Stubblefield told the group the things to look for in the house—that there were lots of repairs to be made. "The house has a mind of its own, you know. You have to make it think it's getting its way."

An attendant came to get Mrs. Stubblefield for lunch and Frances hugged her and told her she would be back soon. Mrs. Stubblefield took her face in her hands and looked her in the eye and told her, "I can tell you are going to be very special to me."

Frances felt she was walking on a springboard as they went to the car. They were all silent on the ride back to the property. Joseph led the way up the drive and pulled to a stop near the front door. They all got out of the cars and stood looking around. Even with the month's neglect, the place was still beautiful. The grounds were spacious, and it was easy to tell that at one time the place was magnificent. They walked around the outside of the house and enjoyed the beautiful shrubs and flower beds. Nadine commented, "Don't you know the Morris boys are going to enjoy playing here."

The group walked up the steps to the porch. Joseph shook the banister that Mrs. Stubblefield had mentioned. The porch went all across the front and the windows came down almost to the floor. There were louvered shutters at the windows. Huge rocking chairs stood as silent reminders of the past owners who had spent evenings resting on the porch before the era of televisions and malls.

Peggy touched the ferns and remarked that they must have received enough rain that had blown in to keep them alive, but that she would water them before leaving. Everyone was touching the columns and windows with reverence as they inspected the neglect of the past few years. They could easily see why Mrs. Stubblefield wanted the place restored.

When Joseph took the key from his pocket, they lined up in silence to enter the house. As they came into the large hall, they stood side by side, surveying the interior. It was if they were afraid that by speaking they would break the spell. The wide circular staircase held a runner that showed the path of the many years of feet ascending to the upper floors. To the right was the parlor, with a rug in the center that matched the runner. Frances noticed that the room was not furnished with all the pieces one might expect. She wondered if Mrs. Stubblefield had disposed of some of the furnishings in order to keep the house.

As she looked around, she thought, *How many homes belong to people who have to sacrifice their beautiful family heirlooms in order to survive?* She vowed that the income from the house would help keep Mrs. Stubblefield comfortable in her new home.

She opened the double pocket doors to a paneled library. It appeared that most of the collection had survived. She could not see vacant spots that would indicate there had been a sacrifice in this room. Mrs. Stubblefield probably valued her library too much. She probably loved the books that had entertained her over the years. Frances touched the heavy draperies that hung on the windows. Although the linings had sustained some damage from the light, the fabric still looked good and could probably be relined. They really did a lot for the room. It would be a shame to lose them.

She turned to look for the rest of the party. They had gathered in the room on the other side of the hall from the parlor. There was a large table in the center of the room, but the chairs and other pieces were missing. There was no other furniture in the other rooms on the first floor.

They opened a door to a rear porch. True to southern architecture, the kitchen must have been separate from the other part of the house, in case of fire. Joseph opened the door to the separate structure, and they found this must have been where Mrs. Stubblefield had been living. The large room had her bed at one side and on the other was her sitting area in front of a large fireplace. A large chair with an ottoman was placed near the window, a beautiful crocheted afghan draped across one arm. On the walls were large pictures of people who were probably Mrs. Stubblefield's family.

Next to the bedroom was a large kitchen. Sitting on a table next to the wall was a hotplate. On the other side was a small table with two cane-bottomed chairs. A white tablecloth with small yellow embroidered flowers decorated the table, with a napkin to match. Joseph was opening the doors of the huge wood stove.

They secured the doors to the rooms and went to inspect the upper floors. They found them also empty of furnishings. It was all so depressing. No wonder Mrs. Stubblefield had been worried about her home. She was running out of furniture to sell, did not want to sell her books, yet probably had no other way to keep the house.

As everyone was getting into the cars to leave, Joseph told her he would see her on Sunday. She got a glimpse of the slight smiles on the faces of the other three women. They were quiet going back to the church.

Chapter 13

The Morris boys' truck was parked at the barn, so they headed out the path to meet them at the door. Nadine smiled. "You two are going to really be happy. Wait until you see the place. As they say in the classified ads, it's a handyman's home."

The two men's eyes twinkled, and they were obviously anxious to hear all the details. Frances said, "This means we're going to have to double our efforts. We need proceeds from the sale to help pay for the house and restoration and then we're going to have to work on that house! This easy country living is going to kill me."

They spent the rest of the day listing items on the computer and packing them for shipment. Otis and Sam asked one question after another. It was obvious they could not wait to get started. Nadine remembered she forgot to water the ferns. Otis and Sam said they would go by on their way home and take care of them. Frances told them she would get the key from Joseph on Sunday and they could see the inside.

That evening during dinner, they worked out a time frame that the group thought would be possible to finish the projects. Sam said they might be able to transfer several items from the church to the house and that would free up space for her to spread out. Frances thought for a moment. "You know, I have begun to like my compact living. It doesn't take a lot to clean and you don't have a lot of places to lose anything. The cats have plenty of room to wander, they seem happy. You have adjusted to eating on the porch. I guess we could get a place to sit when it's cool."

Thinking of the cats, she looked around. Each one of them had selected a lap to sleep in. They really had it made. They were the center of attention.

When the last of the cars had left, Frances took her bath and went to bed. She could not stop thinking about Mrs. Stubblefield and her home. Finally, she pulled on her robe and walked in the dark out to the porch. Stretching out on the lounge, she was immediately joined by the three cats. Positioning themselves around her, they immediately went back to sleep.

Frances leaned her head back and thought again about all that had happened during the past months. Some minutes later, she was awakened by the three cats raising their heads. Not moving, she looked out across the yard. She could not put a finger on what bothered her, whether it was the action of the cats or something else.

Star slipped off the lounge, assuming a low crouch. She eased her way over to the screen and stared out into the darkness. Frances watched the cat and tried to see what she was seeing. Zeus and Sunshine joined Star in her vigilance. There was not a sound to be heard. Obviously, there was something that could not been seen by human eyes, and Frances trusted the cats. She could almost hear her heart beating. She was afraid if she moved to the telephone she would frighten off whatever was out there. She wanted to know what was going on, but what was she going to say to someone anyway? *My cats think they see or hear something.*

After what seemed an eternity, Frances finally saw a slight movement out near the woods. Almost immediately, she saw another figure moving in the darkness. The two figures stopped beside each other and stood for a few moments. Then they moved a few feet and stopped again. Frances could not tell if they were headed toward the house or the barn.

Frances looked at the cats. They were so close to the floor their chins were almost touching. Their tails were wrapped around their bodies and their ears laid back. The three resembled statues. Afraid if she moved, her position on the porch would be detected, her heart beat so hard she could feel the force against her chest. Star began a low growl, then Frances immediately heard a low hiss. At first, she thought it was from one of the cats until she noticed their reaction. They looked over to the side of the building toward the shrubs in the small garden.

Was there another person already at the house? If so, why did the cats not run? Frances looked again in the direction where she had seen the two figures. They were now within forty yards of her. She tried to look around without moving to see if she could reach something to use as a weapon. There was not a thing. Anyway, by the time she jumped off the lounge and attempted to use an object, one of the intruders would reach her. The cats were still watching the two figures.

One of the figures stepped on a twig, and it made a cracking sound. Suddenly, they both dropped to the ground. The cats jumped at the sound. Sunshine looked back as if he would like to run, but was afraid to leave the other two. After a few moments, the two figures again assumed their crouching position and started moving toward the house. Frances closed her eyes and began to pray. She realized that in just a minute, they would be on the porch and she would be seen. Would they shoot her immediately, or would they try to find out if she had money? Either way, she prayed it would be fast and painless.

A voice boomed out of the darkness, and at the same time, a bright light came on, illuminating the figures. This scared Frances, so she let out a cry. At the same time, all three cats ran for the kitchen door. The sheriff called out in a sarcastic voice, "Nice of you gentlemen to come visiting. If you'd called ahead, we would have planned a celebration. Frances, you ring Mary and tell her to call the county. I talked to them today and told them I might need some help."

Frances's legs were so weak that when she stood she didn't think she would be able to walk. The first telephone she reached was in the kitchen and she dialed "O" with a finger that was so shaky she could hardly control it. While waiting, she flipped on the switches and turned on the outside lights. Mary answered soon and Frances gave her the message as she was instructed.

When she hung up the telephone, she walked back out on the porch. The sheriff was standing with a big shotgun pointed at the two figures who were standing with their hands against the side of the garage and their legs spread. When he saw her come back out on the porch, he asked, "Are you all right?"

When Frances spoke, her voice was as shaky as her legs. "I th-think so. How long have you been here?"

"I was already in position when you came out to the porch. I was afraid those detective cats would give my position away. I guess they're so used to me being around they didn't think it was strange that I was lying in the bushes."

Frances went out and sat down on the step. The two men glanced at each other and then over their shoulders at the sheriff. Frances was afraid they would try to overpower him, and she didn't know the extent of his training or if he could handle the two men.

When she heard the sound of the car coming up the lane, Frances could feel her body relax. The car pulled up in front of the garage and a young man got out. He walked over to the sheriff with a nod of his head. "See you caught your suspects." He removed a set of handcuffs from his belt, and while restraining the first man, he started reading them their rights. Before he could get cuffs on the second man, they saw more lights coming up the lane. Three cars and the Morris boys' truck pulled up behind the county car.

Everyone got out and hurried over to Frances. She could see the worried expressions on their faces. They came up beside her and, without a word, turned to watch the officers with the intruders. The sheriff reached into their pockets and pulled out their wallets. He flipped the first one open and looked at the driver's license. "Why, you fellows came all the way from Atlanta to spend time with us. Now isn't that interesting."

Another car pulled around to the garage. It was another police car and two uniformed men got out. Frances turned to go inside. She didn't care what time it was, she was going to make a pot of coffee. There was no way she'd be able to sleep tonight anyway. Her band of friends followed her inside with no one saying a word. As if she could read her mind, Doris reached for the coffeepot and others started getting cups and saucers out of the cabinet.

Frances saw Sam and Otis crouched beside the table in the corner petting the cats. The trio was still not ready to come out. Everyone sat down around one of the tables and waited for the coffee to make. When it made its last gurgle, Mark got up and poured coffee in each of their cups. Occasionally, someone would look toward to door to see if anything was going on outside.

They heard two engines start and then the sheriff came into the kitchen. He sat down with the group and told them what little they had found out. The county was taking the felons over to Marshland to the jail. Someone had hired them to come here to find out what was on the property and then come back and report.

Frances asked, "Do you think the place is safe? I don't mean am I safe, I'm talking about the antiques. I would hate to have them stolen after we've worked so hard and have so many plans to use them, especially since I've met Mrs. Stubblefield. I feel she needs the funds we can provide to help her. I'm sure there are others as desperate for help."

Nadine was first to speak. "I don't think you should be here alone. One of us should stay with you at all times."

"I can't interrupt your lives anymore than I already have. You have dedicated your every waking minute to help me. Anyway, this place is not set up properly. I only have the one bath." Frances was close to tears.

Sam stood and said that wasn't a big problem. "We can fix another bedroom and bath on the other side of the hall. It won't take that long. We'll need to pick up the fixtures. We can probably have it ready by tomorrow night, with the exception of the plumbing. They will have to rough it for one night."

Doris said she would stay. "Frances and I can share the bath without a problem."

Ron said, "Peggy and I can stay the next night. I've never slept in a church before." They all laughed.

"You sleep in church every Sunday," she told him. "Poor Reverend Nolan has learned to overlook you."

Nadine yawned, and everyone started picking up their cups and stacking them in the sink. "We can wash them in the morning."

After the cars left, Doris and Frances locked the door, checked all the windows, and finally lay down on the bed. They did not bother to remove anything but their shoes. Frances lay in the dark, staring at nothing.

Doris asked, "Did you call Joseph?"

After a pause, she said, "No, I'm going to have to learn to deal with my own problems. I can't expect him to run every time something happens to me."

"I think he's going to be hurt if you don't tell him," Doris replied.

Frances thought, *This is the first time I've been on my own my whole life. At first my family protected me, and then Joseph took over.* She felt the tears start to run down her face. There was no way she wanted Doris to see her cry. She felt Doris's hand reach over and pat her arm.

Chapter 14

It was barely daylight when the telephone rang. Doris was the first one up. She glanced over her shoulder. "No." Listening again. "Call Mary, she'll know." After she hung up, she went over to the sink and started a pot of coffee.

Frances struggled to get into the bathroom. She felt as if she'd been through a long illness. In addition to being tired, she was dizzy and nauseated. Taking a cloth and running cold water over it, she placed it on her face. When she removed the cloth and looked in the mirror, she had dark circles under each eye. Making her way back to the bed, she eased herself back down and placed the cloth on her face again. Star curled up next to her and began to purr.

Doris came back to the door when she saw her. "Are you going to be all right?"

Frances lifted the cloth and said she must have come down with a virus. "Why don't you go home? We all need a day off, and I don't want to make you sick." She had expected an argument, but Doris turned and went out the door without a word.

Frances could feel the tears starting again. At least, no one would be around to see her. She finally dozed.

She had not heard a car or the door opening, but she felt someone put their hand on her forehead. "Frances…"

She felt herself smiling. "Joseph, isn't it a beautiful day? The beach is so pretty."

The hand moved down her face. "Frances, we're not at the beach. We're at the church. Are you awake?"

Frances tried to open her eyes, but they did not want to cooperate. She tried to speak again, but her mouth was suddenly dry. She could feel someone moving away from the bed. She could hear the water running in the basin, and in a few minutes, a fresh cloth was placed on her head. She wanted to open her eyes and see who was there, but dozed off to sleep.

The sound of someone in the kitchen woke her sometime later, and then she heard Joseph near her. "Are you going to wake up again? Nadine and Peggy brought some soup for you. Can you try to sit up and eat?" He put his arm beneath her and slid extra pillows to prop her up. Nadine brought in a bowl and a towel to spread over her to catch the drops. Joseph took the spoon and held a bite to her mouth. Frances realized she was hungry and the soup was great. When she had eaten most of the soup, she realized that the room was getting darker. "What time is it?"

Joseph looked at his watch. "Almost eight."

"At night?" Frances asked.

"When you sleep all day, it goes faster," he said with a smile.

Frances heard a car start and leave. "Those girls are so sweet. I don't know what I did to deserve so many friends."

"You were your natural self. That's why you have so many friends. You always think of others rather than yourself. Like this property—you didn't think, 'Look how rich I am,' you thought, 'What can I do for others?'"

Frances thought for a minute, but she could not see herself in that manner. She had thought of herself as being self-centered in the past. Living her life and not worrying for others.

Joseph asked if she felt like taking a bath. "Am I that bad?" she wanted to know.

"No, I just thought it would make your muscles feel better," he replied with a slight poke.

She heard him in the bathroom running water into the tub. Pulling herself out of bed, she went to the chest to find clean clothes. When she went into the bathroom, he had lit candles. "Thank you, this is great."

When he went out the door, she settled into the warm water. She could hear him talking with the cats and giving them treats. He was right, she was already feeling better. She remembered Doris's conversation on the telephone. That was why she did not argue with her when she suggested she go home. She, Peggy, and Nadine were plotting to get Joseph here with her. That was what Doris meant when she said Mary would know. Mary would know Joseph's telephone number. *They are so sneaky*, thought Frances with a smile, *and am I glad*.

When she came out of the bathroom, Joseph was just finishing changing the sheets on the bed. He pulled back the covers and motioned for her to lie down. The cats had already positioned themselves at the foot of the bed. When she crawled back beneath the covers, he pulled them up and gave her a little pat. "You were right, I do feel better," she said weakly.

Joseph sat down in the chair beside the bed and started talking about the renovations of Mrs. Stubblefield's house. He had been thinking a lot about the possibilities, and as he talked, Frances was visualizing what he was saying. Before she knew it, she was asleep again.

Sometime during the night, she woke and the room was dark. Star was curled up next to her stomach. She started rubbing her and realized she could hear someone breathing. She rose up on one elbow, looking toward the chair, and in the dim light coming from the window, she could tell it was empty. Looking back over her shoulder, she could see the shape of Joseph on the other side of the bed, with Zeus and Sunshine against him. What would people think when they found out he had spent the night here? Lying back down, she decided she couldn't care less. She was not doing anything wrong.

At the first light of day, she slipped out of bed and dressed. When her coffee was ready, she went out to the porch. She had not been there long when she heard Joseph pouring himself a cup of coffee and heading to the porch. He smiled as he came out and took another lounge. "I see why you like this porch."

They sat side by side without saying anything. The birds were performing their usual symphony. After a while, Joseph asked, "Do you feel like riding into town and getting everyone and going out to the house?"

"Yes, I am really anxious to see it again. It's still like a dream. I know the Morris boys are anxious to see the inside."

Joseph got up and went out to his car. He retrieved the spare clothes he had in the trunk and got his traveling shaving kit. Going back inside, he told her that he would just be a minute.

When he was ready, they closed the doors and turned on the alarm. He opened the door for her and she settled into the seat. This really felt strange. The interior of the car was silent as they drove into town. As they passed the service station, Frances saw the sheriff stand up to look out. Joseph drove around to the residential street and pulled up in front of the Morris boys' house. They were sitting on the porch in their chairs. When they recognized them, they smiled and came down the steps to greet them.

Joseph, getting out of the car, shook their hands and asked if they would like to ride out to see the house. Otis said they could not wait. Frances got out and started over to Nadine's house. Before she was halfway across the street, she saw all three women coming out of their houses and heading to Doris's car. She turned back and said, "I think they are ready."

The house held its same mystery and allure as before. Frances stood in front looking up and felt small compared to the trees and the tall porch. Everyone else had gone inside, and she was wandering around in the yard. There was so much to see on the property. Everywhere she looked, she could visualize the possibilities. She walked up the rear steps to the porch and could hear everyone in the center hall discussing the architecture and sharing their ideas. When she went inside, Joseph was saying, "I spoke with Mrs. Stubblefield's attorney and he was sure they could have the paperwork finished in three weeks and we could sign it."

Frances picked up on the "we could sign." She had not thought about this. Did he want to own the property jointly? She thought that since she was not employed, it could be a handicap in trying to borrow money to buy this place. How did Joseph think the situation would work after he went home? She guessed she would make the payments, maintain the upkeep, and settle with him at the end of the year. She noticed the others' glancing from her to each other. She guessed they had as many questions as she did.

Sam and Otis had started jotting notes in little pads they carried in their pockets. Frances could tell they could not wait to get started. If any two people enjoyed restoration, these two men did. She wondered if they had done the work on the homes on their street.

In the middle of the afternoon, they headed back to Synaxis, dropped off Sam and Otis, then headed back to the church.

Joseph asked her if she would like to eat something, and she told him she was beginning to feel hungry. When they went in, they immediately headed to the refrigerator to see what they could salvage to eat.

Later, Frances and Joseph were resting on the lounges and the cats had divided between them. Frances could tell from the expression on Joseph's face that he wanted to say something, but could not figure out how to start. They had been silent for a long time when he cleared his throat and began, "I know I've made a lot of mistakes, but I've had time to think about where I went wrong. I couldn't open up to you, and suddenly, I felt I was being unfair to both of us. When you left town, my life was so empty I couldn't stay there any longer. At first, I thought I just wanted to see you once again, but when I did, I knew I could not live without you. I understand your bitterness, but I know you understand how the pressure had built inside me. I no longer felt I was an architect, but a draftsperson designing—no, not designing—just drawing what people wanted to see. I could no longer see the visions like I did before. It didn't take me long in those few days after I saw you here to know what I wanted. I have to have a life with you. You give me my inspiration. When I saw you could be happy here in this setting, I knew I was the half of the marriage that had quit trying. Will you give me another chance?"

"Joseph, are you sure you could live like this? I am so happy that I can contribute to mankind around me. I don't mean vast amounts of money, just share the part of myself with them to help them along. There is an empty place in my life that only you can fill. No matter how many friends were around me, I still was missing something. When you're here, that emptiness goes away. I don't want you to rush into anything. You need to be sure you're making the right decision—I cannot go through the hurt again."

Joseph looked at her and spoke slowly. "I'm not rushing. The minute you walked onto this porch that first time, I knew in my heart I had made a mistake and I wanted more than anything to take you in my arms and ask you to take me back. We need each other. Our lives were too full before to throw away. I know that now. I'm sure in three weeks, we can have everything ready to repeat our vows, if you agree."

Frances did not answer at first. She looked out at the yard and the flowers that were beginning to grow and at the spots where the grass was beginning to turn green again. She thought of how it would be to share this place with Joseph. He was right; their life together had been wonderful. She did not want to lose him again. With him at her side, this place could be all she could ever want. "Yes, Joseph, I think that would be wonderful."

Joseph's eyes were moist as he got up, came over, and sat beside her on the lounge. Taking her in his arms, he held her close. Kissing her gently on the lips, he said, "I love you so very much and always will."

After Joseph had left, Frances sat up in bed and told the cats she was going to have a surprise for them real soon.

Chapter 15

Everyone gathered early the next morning at the barn to work. They had fallen behind schedule and were trying to catch up. Mark had found a covered truck with a hydraulic tailgate. They had rearranged their tables so it could be put in the barn at night for security. Sam and Otis built some shelves on one side for small items with nets to keep items from falling while traveling.

All morning, Frances wanted to tell everyone her good news, but knew she should wait for Joseph to share the event. He said he would bring dinner for everyone tonight and to be sure to have everyone present. She would catch herself smiling while she was working and glanced up to see several watching her with raised eyebrows.

When the day finally ended and they had closed the barn, she almost ran to the house. Joseph was still unloading the food when she arrived and she helped him finish. He was smiling at her and it was as if no one else existed in the world. She turned with a box and caught the women with their heads together whispering. The cats were chasing around the room, having the time of their life, jumping on the backs of the lounges, and pouncing on each other.

When everyone was ready to eat, James led the prayer while they held hands. Everyone was almost finished eating when Doris laid down her fork and asked, "When are you two going to tell us what is going on?" There was total silence.

Joseph finally spoke. "I have asked Frances to renew her vows with me. We have had a long talk and think we know where it went wrong." There were screams of glee and everyone was talking at the same time. You could hear a few words out of the turmoil: "When?" "Where?"

Joseph said he wanted to do it as soon as possible. Naturally, the ceremony would be here at the property. They would get the necessary papers and speak to the minister. Next week would be a good time.

If anyone in the world enjoyed excitement and planning, this group led the list. The women had already started their list of things they needed to get ready and the men had gone outside to select the perfect spot. Frances looked up and saw Joseph standing in the middle of the porch looking from one group to another. Finally, he started outside to "help" the men. They were in the middle of the meditation garden walking around arranging the seating and flowers. Sam and Otis were at one corner, discussing what kind of arch they could build. Ron and Mark were pacing off the area to see how many chairs could be placed.

Doris, Nadine, and Peggy had moved out onto the driveway in front of the garage and were planning placement of tables for food.

Frances and Joseph walked away from the groups and headed for the cemetery. As they walked around, Frances noticed that more work had been done. Most of the markers had been cleaned and all the weeds had been pulled. On several of the graves, fresh flowers had been planted. Joseph was standing in an area that did not have any graves. He paced around, looking at the ground and the surrounding area. He finally turned toward Frances and asked what she thought about putting a bench for people to use when they were visiting. Frances agreed that it would be a good idea. It would reinforce the feeling that they did not have to hurry but were welcome.

As they walked back to the house, they could hear the commotion from the porch with everyone giving their ideas. Frances and Joseph looked at each other and laughed. "This is going to be worse than the first time. We thought we were going to have a *small* ceremony!"

Nadine said they would take care of everything. All Frances and Joseph had to do was show up at the right time. Frances asked, "Have you set the time?"

They all laughed, and Nadine said, "Of course."

"As long as you're taking care of everything, you'll have to show me where I can buy a new dress," Frances said, realizing she had not purchased anything for herself in over a year.

The group started gathering all their notes, then said their good-byes, and left. The porch was silent for a few minutes. The three cats were still sitting at the edge of the porch staring out at the evening shadows. Frances and Joseph were enjoying the peace of the moment.

"Are you driving over to Marshland tomorrow?" Joseph asked as he reached for her hand.

Frances turned her head in the semi-darkness and studied his profile. "I'm looking forward to the trip. I think the cats are getting bored, and they will enjoy the outing. I plan to leave early so I can see the sunrise over the water."

She could barely see Joseph's smile. "In that case, I'll have us a picnic breakfast prepared. I have a balcony that faces east that will be perfect. The cats can see their first ocean-view sunrise. I'll watch for you so I can help you carry the cats up the stairs."

He leaned over and gave her a kiss on the cheek and got up from his chair. Frances followed him over to the screen door and latched it after he left. She leaned against the frame and watched him pull out of the driveway. Star got up and wound her body around Frances's legs. Frances reached down to pick her up and enjoy her song. The cat snuggled close as Frances went inside, with the other two cats following close behind.

Chapter 16

When the alarm went off the next morning, Frances started dressing and the cats sat side by side watching her through half-open eyes. When she got their carriers, they immediately sprang to life. Frances always thought it was unusual that each cat had always gone to its own special carrier. They were inside and ready to go without a word from her. She loaded them in the backseat of her car and went back to set the alarm.

She had never been to town when it was dark. As she passed the homes, there were few lights showing. She slowed her car as she neared Mrs. Stubblefield's home. She could still not believe that soon, they could start restoration of this beautiful old place. "You three look out the window to the right. See that big house? You are going to get to go inside. You will really like the place. It has lots of hiding places, stairs to run up and down, and big windows to look outside." She glanced at the three cats and saw they were looking at the house as if they understood what she was saying. She finally resumed her speed. "We better hurry—don't want to miss sunrise."

Joseph must have seen her car coming because he was at her door when she stopped. Opening the car door, he embraced her and gave her a kiss on the forehead. All three cats were voicing their opinions that it was time to get out of the car. Joseph took the two carriers containing Zeus and Sunshine and Frances pulled Star's carrier from the other side of the car. Joseph had already taken his load upstairs and had come back to help her with Star.

As soon as they were inside with the door closed, Joseph released the cats and they started their investigation. Joseph led Frances to a table on the balcony where he had prepared a beautiful breakfast. He had used a white tablecloth, complete with flowers. They sat at the table angled so both could enjoy the view. As they ate, they watched the horizon become brighter. When the sun appeared, Frances said in a breathless voice, "That is so beautiful!

Movement at the railing caught their eye. Three heads poked through a rail and each cat was watching the sunrise. When they became tired of the view, they made their way to a lounge and went back to sleep.

Joseph showed Frances the plans for the development. He was proud of the preservation of the area. The buildings were placed to enhance the island and not turn it into a commercial eyesore. He had the spirit and enthusiasm that had attracted her to him. His blue eyes would sparkle as he talked.

Joseph suggested they load the cats and go for a ride. When it was obvious they were going somewhere, all three cats went to their carriers. They had agreed to go in Frances's car since she had the boxes and straps so the cats could ride safely and see outside. When the strap was pulled secure to keep the carriers from tilting forward, Joseph opened the door for Frances and went around to the driver side of the car. "Are you sure you can drive my antique?" she asked, smiling.

Joseph pointed out the different landmarks of the area and explained the history of each. He stopped at one beach and took time to unload each carrier and set it down on the sand near the water. At first, the cats laid back their ears and did not appear to like their first trip to the beach. Finally, Sunshine extended his paw through the opening and grabbed at the water when it came near him. Next, Star extended her paw through the opening and touched the sand. When she drew it back inside, it was obvious that she did not like it sticking to the bottom of her foot. She gave it a firm shake and kept it inside.

Joseph drove over the bridge to the island to show Frances its progress. He explained that he had located a horticulturist to help with the plants, which partially explained their beauty. "I want him to visit Mrs. Stubblefield's home and help us get the plants and trees reestablished. I've already mentioned it to him and he's excited that he's going to be able to help us with the project."

Joseph pulled over to a restaurant that had outside picnic tables in the shade. They unloaded the cats onto one of the benches, and he went inside to order the plates to bring outside. The cats feasted on fish, while Joseph and Frances each enjoyed a pulled pork barbeque sandwich with all the trimmings, Southern style. Frances watched the cats' long pink tongues savoring the traces of their lunch on their whiskers.

"What do you think about heading back to the church and stopping on the way to look at the house again?" Joseph asked as he cleared the tables. "I can't get enough of the place."

Frances looked up at him. "I would love to! I know the cats will love prowling."

Joseph drove back to get his car and she followed him to the old house. When she slowed to make the turn into the driveway, the cats stretched their necks to see both sides of the drive. When she pulled up beside Joseph, he could hear all three cats in their cries of excitement. He had parked near the rear of the house so it would be easier to transport the carriers inside.

Once inside, the three cats were released and at first started a slow investigation of the house. They would go from room to room checking out each window and corner, but never leaving sight of each other. When they had finished a room to their satisfaction, they would move to another. Frances and Joseph noticed they spent a long time in the library. They would sniff books, chairs, lamps, and Star even stood on her back legs and peered into the wastebasket. Joseph and Frances never tired of watching the cats. Every day was different.

When Frances and Joseph started up the stairs, they heard the sound of small feet running toward them. They were past halfway up by all three cats running as fast as possible. When they reached the landing, they slid on the hardwood, trying to make the turn. Upstairs, they chased from room to room and back down the hall several times before finding Frances and starting their inspection of the second floor.

Joseph was checking the water tanks in the bathrooms to see what repairs were going to be necessary. Frances opened a closet in one room and found a beautiful vintage wedding dress sealed in a protective box. As she looked at it, she could not believe the detail of the pearls on the bodice. The high collar was stitched with the same detail. This would be beautiful to display in a case downstairs.

At the end of the hall, Frances opened a door and found a flight of steps going to an attic. Although the steps were steep and narrow, she placed her hand on the banister and started to ascend slowly. When she got far enough up the stairs so she could look through the banister, she paused to look around the space. As her eyes were adjusting to the dim light, a wail sounded behind her. Jumping, she almost lost her balance. "Star! Why do you always scare me?" In her way of apology, Star rubbed Frances's ankle before she passed to investigate the new space. Just as she started to sniff a box, Frances said, "Psssst!" causing Star to jump. "See how it feels?"

When Frances got to the top of the stairs, she saw Zeus and Sunshine slowly coming up the stairs. Frances could see trunks and boxes filling the room. There were odds and ends of furniture that needed repair. Frances opened one of the trunks and found old clothing—several beautiful old dresses from many years ago. She did not take them out, but gently moved them to see what else was inside. In one trunk, she found a beautiful black silk dress with a high neckline and large puffy sleeves. This must have been someone's mourning dress. Beside the dress was a small pair of black high-top lace-up shoes. Frances could not imagine anyone with such small feet. She picked up the waist of the mourning dress and saw again a small opening.

She heard Joseph's voice from downstairs. "Frances, where are you?" All three cats went over to the edge of the landing and peered down. Zeus gave his throaty meow and Joseph came up the stairs. "What have you found?" He knelt beside her and peered inside the trunk.

"Joseph, this is beautiful. I wonder if we could get some display cases to put downstairs or perhaps throughout the house for people to enjoy them—yet they would be protected." Joseph ran his hand over the fabric and picked up one of the shoes. "I really don't see why not."

They closed the trunk and stood up to look around. "It will probably take several weeks just to go through all the cases and inventory what's here. But we'll need to get more lighting. Everyone is going to have a great time working on this project."

Frances and Joseph made their way over to the stairs and called the cats. Star and Sunshine came immediately. They could hear Zeus making his was over to them, and from the sound, they knew he was bringing something with him. "I hope it isn't a rodent," Frances prayed aloud as Zeus came nearer. When he came out from between two boxes, he had a small book in his mouth. Frances knelt down and took it from him. It was bound with a soft cover and was very old. When she opened it, she found small neat handwriting, probably belonging to one of the females who lived in the house. She told Zeus, "Thank you."

Chapter 17

Monday morning brought all of her friends out to the church. If she thought they were going to work on the antiques, she was mistaken. They had sketches, lists, and were giving orders like marine sergeants. Sam and Otis were in the garden working on seating and unloading the tables they had purchased to sort the antiques and were bringing them into the garage to use for food tables in the driveway. The women were searching boxes, looking for linens and serving pieces. They were methodically checking boxes and would occasionally move a box into one of the rooms where they were grouping the antiques.

Naturally, all three cats were helping. When one of the women finished looking in a box, they would have to remove a cat before closing the top. After a few searches, the cats became bored and started chasing each other over the tops of the boxes, seeing which could jump the highest.

When the women had made all their selections, they grouped everything in the garage and sat down to go over their lists. Frances was told they would go out to purchase her attire that afternoon. She thought to herself, *Now, that should be an adventure*. The food plans were different. They were going to have covered dishes. Frances wanted to know, "What is a covered dish?"

They explained that everyone brought a dish of their favorite food. It was popular at church socials. Frances asked, "How many are you expecting?"

"Just a few of the town's people," Nadine said, winking. Frances knew from their actions and sideways glances at each other that they were up to something.

That afternoon, they all loaded into Doris's van and headed to Marshland. The shop they had selected was small, but unique. It had been so long since Frances had shopped for clothes that she just stood in the middle of the floor for a few minutes, staring around trying to decide where she should start. The other four women were working the racks. They each selected an armload of dresses and the owner of the shop took them to her largest fitting room and the show began. All of their selections would have been perfect. Frances wondered how on earth she would make a decision. She had decided that she would not look at any of the prices; the decision would be made on what she liked best.

After she had tried on dresses from each of their selections, she wondered how she would make a selection without hurting one person's feelings. The owner of the shop came in with a dress over her arm. When she held it up for Frances to see, all five women gave their approval. When Frances slipped the dress over her head and someone zipped it up the back, she turned to the mirror. The dress was a soft peach lace. The neck was perfect. As she turned to look at herself, they all sucked in a breath, but no one said a word. She finally held up her arms and asked, "Well, what do you think?"

There was a unanimous: "Perfect."

On the way back home, Doris told her, "We'll keep the dress in town so Joseph won't see it before the wedding. Do you have special jewelry you would like to wear?"

Frances thought for a moment. "Yes, I want to wear the pearls my parents gave me on my wedding day."

Her friends had helped her transform the kitchen to a beautiful room. Furniture had been pulled from various places and arranged in groupings. Someone had found a large light fixture and installed it, casting soft lighting over the room. When the new curtains had been installed, they all stood back to admire. "We're so glad you moved to town, Frances. We were running out of projects to keep us out of trouble."

When Frances heard this remark, she replied, "I think we can all stay busy for a long time with all we've taken on."

The day of the wedding was there before Frances could believe it. If she had told her friends from a few years ago how her life had changed, they would never believe her. When she woke up that morning, the cats were all over the bed, staring at her like a child on Christmas morning, waiting for her to get up. Frances wondered how on earth they knew something special was going to happen. Every day was an adventure for them. She no longer worried about their wanderings through the buildings.

From time to time, Frances had found small objects in the kitchen or bedroom that had been transported there by Zeus. They were always things that she enjoyed. How he found the objects was still a mystery. One evening when she started to bed, she found a key in the middle of the bed. She picked it up and examined the small object. It was not one she had seen before and it was obviously old. She looked at the cats as if to ask where it came from, but all she got were stares. She put the key away, thinking someday she would find the lock it opened.

During the time she was getting ready for the wedding, Frances could hear the preparations being made outside. She did not dare look outside for fear of being overwhelmed. Anyway, her friends kept saying they wanted to surprise her.

When the four women tapped on her door and she opened it, they all rushed in to see how she looked. There were *ooohs* and *aaaahs* from everyone. She was doing her spin in the middle of the floor, and she suddenly stopped. "I just realized the cats have not been in here with me."

Peggy said, "Don't you worry, they are being cared for."

Music and chatter could be heard from outside. It was all Frances could do not to look out the window. Doris finally spoke up, "Well, it's show time!"

The four women led the way out the door to the outside. When Frances saw the transformation of the garden, she could not believe her eyes. There were about seventy-five people gathered for the happy occasion. Joseph stood near a beautiful arch, alongside Reverend Nolan. Sitting on a high perch were three screen cages holding the cats, all three sporting new collars and peering down at everyone. Zeus was sporting a white collar with a tiny bow tie at the back. Sunshine had a black collar with a bow tie, and Star had a silver collar with peach buds at the back of the head. Frances wondered how on earth they managed to persuade the cats to adjust.

Their vows were spoken with the singing of the birds. When the ceremony was completed, everyone gathered around giving their best wishes. When the food was ready and the blessing had been offered, Frances feasted on the best food she had ever tasted. She wanted to try it all.

Everyone was having a great time. There was a constant parade of groups walking to and from the cemetery and just milling around the old church admiring its beauty. Frances heard comments from people who were wondering why the property had just been forgotten. Others were saying how happy they were to be able to enjoy themselves in the history of the place. Everyone promised to come back and help with the maintenance of the cemetery.

Frances tried to retain the names of the people she had met that day. Each person seemed sincerely glad they had been included in the festivities. These were people she wanted to get to know better. She wondered how she could have spent as much time in Synaxis and not encountered them before. This too was going to change.

Mysteriously, all the tables, chairs, food, and evidence of the day quickly disappeared and the yard looked normal again. As the last of the cars drove away, Frances and Joseph stood side by side, watching them leave. The three cats were sitting on the porch waiting for them.

Chapter 18

Early the next week, work resumed on getting the inventory ready to take to the auction. Everyone was motivated and had a mission. They made more progress than they had ever made before. It was as if nothing was holding them back.

The day before the scheduled date to leave, all items were double checked, the lists were made, and everything was securely loaded into the van. Sam and Otis decided they were going to stay home and watch out for the property. Since they had cleared a lot of the boxes and pieces from the barn, they wanted to go through some of the items in the church and decide what they could put in the loft. Then they would get things arranged so decisions could be made as to what was going to be taken to Mrs. Stubblefield's when the house was ready. They also wanted to start a list of work that needed to be done on the house so they would be ready as soon as the paperwork was completed. "Anyway," Sam said as he stroked the cat that was asleep in his lap, "I don't think the cats need to be dragged away from home."

Frances was relieved. They were going to take Doris's van and the truck. James was not going with them. He said he and the sheriff would watch the town.

When they left town on this trip, there was no fanfare. It was still dark and there were only the two vehicles. Everyone was quiet for a long time until Nadine finally spoke, "Frances, do you feel you're taking one of your children to give them away?"

Frances answered, "Yes, but we have to sacrifice these in order to accomplish what we've set out to do. I hope we'll make enough from this sale to get the house in order and get the museum started. We'll need to lie low for a while. If we start selling too much, people will start asking questions. I don't want to draw attention to us."

When the items were unloaded at the auction house, the owners seemed impressed with the quality and beauty of the antiques. They were asking the same questions as the people in Atlanta had asked and were given basically the same answers. The more exposure Frances got from reaction to the antiques, the more determined she became to protect them. Before they left, she took one last look. She kept reminding herself that this had to be done.

When they returned home, the first problem she encountered was a phone call from the insurance company she had contacted about a policy. They were asking for an inventory and appraisals. That evening, there was a group meeting at the dinner table. Everyone realized this has to be done, but they were nowhere close to having the inventory complete and had completely stopped looking for an appraiser that they felt they could trust. They all agreed that they did not want to work with anyone in Atlanta.

Suddenly, Frances had an idea. "When Mrs. Stubblefield sold her antiques, how did she set a value?" Everyone at the table looked at each other, but no one had an answer. Joseph picked up the telephone and called the nursing home where she was living.

When Mrs. Stubblefield answered her telephone, Joseph told her of their problem. She told him to look in her writing table at a personal book listing all her friends and their telephone numbers. In that book was a Mrs. Williams who lived in Savannah. She had known her for her entire life and knew she could be trusted. Mrs. Stubblefield told them that Mrs. Williams attended all the auctions and was often commissioned to make private appraisals, and that she even used a computer to keep up-to-date.

Their next call was to Mrs. Williams. When she learned the reason for the call, she was ecstatic.

"I will be in Synaxis first thing in the morning."

As they ate the chocolate cake, they decided things were going to work out fine. If Mrs. Stubblefield trusted Mrs. Williams, then they could trust her. Sam and Otis said they had outlined a plan to move the heavy pieces of furniture to Mrs. Stubblefield's as soon as the renovations were complete. J. T. and his sons would be able to help. Since the van had a hydraulic tail gate, they could back up to the front door of the sanctuary and handle the load.

It was also decided that the crates in the basement needed to be investigated to be able to know what pieces could be used. They would start there first thing in the morning.

Chapter 19

Looking like a bunch of refuges from a work camp, they all trudged down the steps carrying crowbars, laptops, bottles of water, and three excited cats. They divided into two groups: Sam with Frances and Doris, Otis with Peggy and Nadine. Each group went to *their* side of the basement and started opening crates.

Otis got his crate open first, and when Peggy and Nadine squealed, all work on the other side stopped and everyone went to see if it was snakes, rats, or what. All six peered inside the crate at what was revealed beneath the cloth that had covered the top item. The cloisonné vases lay sparkling in the reflection of the overhead light. Even the three cats that had run to see the excitement were speechless. It was as if they understood the beauty they were seeing.

Frances finally spoke. "I think we need to regroup. Don't you think we need to get a sorting table and pull everything out, prepare the inventory, repack the crate, and move on to the next crate?" Everyone agreed. "Anyway, no one will get any work done for being afraid of missing something. I know I won't."

After the sorting table and wheel trucks had been brought downstairs, the group walked around and looked at all the crates.

They calculated, based on the number of crates, how long to unpack, count, and repack, that it would take three months. They had started a tracking system using the number that had been placed on the crate in the past. They were walking around the large area, looking and thinking. "We also have the problem of how to get the crates out of the basement after we're finished. We will have to maneuver the crates around so we can check what is inside each one. The way they are stacked, we can't get access."

Sam spoke up. "We have an access on the south side with a storm door opening. You don't notice it because there are shrubs all around it and it doesn't show."We can move some of the plants so we can put the conveyor down the steps and can bring the crates up to the truck. I'm afraid we're going to need additional muscle power. Those crates are heavy, and we're not going to be able to handle them."

They decided to break for lunch and have a conference. Doris made a list of people in town they felt they could rely upon not to discuss their business with *outsiders*.

It was agreed that J. T. and his sons would be first on their list. Otis gave J. T. a call and told him what they needed and asked if their price would be in line. J. T. and his sons were pleased to be included and would be over first thing in the morning.

Frances finally posed a question that had not been mentioned before. "Has anyone thought of the fact that Mrs. Stubblefield's house will not hold all the pieces and be able to maintain the beauty of the place?" There was silence for a few minutes.

Nadine suggested, "Could we loan out some of the pieces to museums? Everyone smiled at the same time, and there was no doubt they were all in agreement. "This is going to require a lot of work. Records will have to be kept, shipping, coordination. This will be a big job."

Frances looked from one to another. "Have I asked too much of you?" The unison of voices from the group was a loud no.

Doris summed it up for them: "Before we became involved with you and your mission, we existed in our day-to-day lives. We all had our love and friendships, we shared our tasks, but something was missing. We have developed fervor for life that we had forgotten. No job is too great."

Peggy said, "I don't think I could give it up at this point. As I said before, the antiques are beginning to feel like a child I need to protect."

Sam had been quiet during the talk, but finally asked, "Do you know who owns the old cotton warehouse down near the railroad tracks?"

Peggy answered, "Ron inherited it from his father. It hasn't been used in years. Minimum maintenance has been done to preserve it, but nothing else. Hey! That would be ideal for storage."

Otis said, "We would need to get security installed and have the roof checked. I guess they are beginning to wonder what on earth we're doing to suddenly need so much security. Do you think if we put a couple of men with guns and guard dogs that would raise some eyebrows?"

Nadine laughed. "No, I think they would expect guard *cats*."

Peggy said she thought there were a few offices in the building. "We could use them to store records and work. We'd need to get telephones installed."

They all loaded into vehicles and set off for town. The warehouse was typical of the early nineteen hundreds. A platform ran the entire length of the building on both sides and had several wide door openings. At the corner of the building near the street was an office area. It had large windows that had served as ventilation before air conditioning. They had stopped at Peggy's to get the key, and she opened the door, which had a squeak from another era. Across the entire room near the front was a counter. A swinging gate was at the far end to discourage people from wandering into the office. Three partner's desks were positioned down the middle of the area, with wooden swivel chairs. The chairs contained cushions covered in fabric of the era. Along the back wall were wooden file cabinets. Each member of the group walked around the room opening file drawers and desk drawers. All appeared to be empty. Beneath the counter was shelving, also empty, with the exception of dust.

Everyone had stopped and brushed their hands together to get rid of as much of the dust as possible. Frances asked, "How much money is in our budget that we can allow for help? There's no way we can continue to do everything. We'll have to have help getting everything in order."

Peggy, who had taken charge of the checkbook, said, "With the money from the sale in Atlanta, you're still in good shape. It shouldn't take more than a couple of thousand to get things in order and start moving everything here. I think this will be much easier on you."

Frances looked at her seriously. "You have made one mistake." No one said a word. She continued, "We *are* in good shape. This could not have been done without all of us. I would still be sleeping on a table in the kitchen and wandering around boxes, following three cats, wondering what I should do."

"Well…" Doris mused with one finger at her cheek. "I would still be sitting in my rocking chair trying to scare people."

It was decided they would recruit Gail, Margaret, Connie, and Louise to help them get the place organized.

Nadine and Peggy went to their stores to get cleaning supplies. When they returned, they were laden with push broom, buckets, dust cloths, polish, and anything else they thought would be necessary.

The telephone and security would be installed the next day. The rest of the day was spent ridding the place of years of dust. A jug of tea and a cooler of ice mysteriously appeared on the counter. No one had to ask where it came from. At six o'clock, the door opened, and Joseph, Ron, Mark, and Doc came in loaded with food boxes. The feast was laid on the counter. They walked around in the building and could not believe the work.

Ron was grateful that the building could once again be used. "My father would be pleased. He spent a lot of hours working here. At one time, this was a hub for the city. If you wanted to know what was happening, you would come here and someone knew all the details."

While they were eating, a game plan was put into place. They needed to get the tables moved from the church. The decided they would call J. T. and his sons and see if they could help for a couple of hours while there were extra men. By seven-thirty, all the men and trucks were headed to get their first load.

While they were gone, the women went to the warehouse and decided the best location for the tables. With chalk, they marked areas for storage on the floor for the different categories.

Gail, Connie, Margaret, and Louise wanted to help with inventory. They certainly did need additional help. They were not under the gun to get the job finished, but the need to get everything listed was urgent. They had decided it would be best to move everything from storage at the church to the warehouse where it could be processed faster.

It was ten o'clock when they locked the door at the warehouse. The procession was moving very slowly. There was no commotion. The good-byes were low and there were a few groans heard when someone got into their vehicle.

Chapter 20

Nadine and Peggy came out to the church the next morning to help Frances. Doris was going to remain at the warehouse with Gail, Connie, Margaret, and Louise.

J. T. and his sons, Don, Kevin, and Jason, as Frances soon learned, had arrived with Sam and Otis at the first sign of sunrise.

Everyone was standing at the back side of the church, looking at the large bushes. Frances had never given them any thought. After thirty minutes of digging and moving, since it was decided it would be a shame to destroy the plants, a large door covering what was an outside entry to the basement was displayed. The two doors were supposed to be raised to open. After many years of never having been opened, this was not an easy task. The operation took another thirty minutes with some of the men going to the basement to push and some on the outside to pull.

Frances could hear periodic cries from the cats since they were not being included in the latest adventure. Everyone would give them a pat when they went near them, but this was not enough.

J. T. had been able to get a portable hoist from someone, and this was going to be used to load the conveyor on the truck and help get the crates from the basement to the conveyor to the truck. Getting this accomplished took hour. Frances looked at her watch. This has taken a lot of time, but from here on out, it would be production.

When the first crate started up the conveyor, someone said, "Mission Control, we have liftoff!"

At four o'clock, they locked up the church headed into town. The progress in the warehouse was unbelievable. They had phones, security, the roof had been given a good bill of health, and between loads, they had cleaned the inside of the file cabinets.

Mrs. Williams had arrived around ten and was excited as a child in a toy store. They had opened a few of the crates, and she was enthusiastic about the beauty and quality of the antiques. She had a lot of suggestions on to how to arrange the items to improve speed and control.

Doris said Mrs. Williams would stay with her while she was in town.

Sam and Otis calculated that about ten percent of the crates in the basement had been moved. They all agreed it would go faster now that everything was in place and they had the *hang* of what to do.

That evening was a replay of the night before. Everyone quietly went home to soak their aching muscles and get ready for another day.

As Frances lay in the large tub soaking, she told the cats that were beside the tub also bathing themselves, "This quiet country living is getting the best of me. What happened to listening to the birds singing and resting in a rocking chair?"

When she went out onto the porch Joseph had two glasses of lemonade ready for them. They sat quietly listening to the night sounds. He reached over and squeezed her hand gently. She turned her head to look at his profile in the semi-darkness. She was so lucky. There was not a thing in the world she could ask for. She hoped God knew how thankful she was for the life he had given her.

Chapter 21

Each day of the following week was a replay of the day before—work, sleep, work. One morning when Frances headed to the warehouse she was sitting at a traffic light waiting for it to change. She had been going over a list in her mind of what she needed to do that day. She suddenly focused on the store fronts ahead of her. The windows had been washed. She could not believe it! There were even planters with flower out front. When had they had time.

When Frances went into the warehouse, she cornered the three women first thing. "What has happened to you? I thought you wanted to keep everyone out?"

Doris appointed herself spokesperson. "We were talking the other night. What if you had not stayed in Synaxis? We would have missed a great opportunity. Have we turned others away that could have made a difference? We decided that we would give a little."

Frances laughed. "Give a little! I woke up in a new town this morning. I could not believe my eyes."

Nadine scoffed. "Am I glad I was not on the streets yesterday morning. I would have been flattened. Did you not open your eyes when you came through town? Girl, you are working too hard."

Mrs. Williams was giving the women a crash course in appraisal. They were learning to read the marks on the bottom of pieces. Everything has a *tattoo*, they were told. You can tell the manufacturer by the marks. Other qualities narrow down the period of the piece.

Later, Mrs. Williams was talking with Frances at one of the sorting tables. "Do you realize the value of the antiques you have?"

Frances was silent for a few minutes, and then she replied, "I know it is beyond my wildest dream. When I went to Atlanta and Ashville, I began to realize what had been left in this town. For what reason, I have not been able to find out. I do know one thing: I do not want—no, let me correct myself—*we* do not want them destroyed or placed in the hands of people who do not appreciate their beauty. We would like to be able to establish a foundation to maintain the collection after we're gone. This is part of history. Future generations need to know where we have come from, and hopefully, the collection will help lead us to a future of people who appreciate our forefathers."

Mrs. Williams patted her on the arm. "I'm glad you were chosen to be responsible."

By the end of the month, the basement had been cleared at the church. Mrs. Williams went out to the church to tour with the group. Frances met them on the porch when they arrived. As they came inside Star, Zeus, and Sunshine had lined up to inspect the newcomers. They remembered most of them from the wedding.

As Mrs. Williams went from room to room, she could not believe the quantity still remaining in the building. They all sat down on the pew while everyone took in the beauty of the sanctuary. When they went to the barn and other storage buildings, Mrs. Williams was speechless.

They decided they should go out to see Mrs. Stubblefield. When they arrived, the reunion between the two old friends was touching. It was interesting to listen to the two ladies tell how they had gone to visit in the old homes of the south.

Mrs. Stubblefield wanted to know about the progress they had made on her house. Frances told her that they wanted her to visit as soon as it was safe for her. Her eyes twinkled when she heard of the paint, planting, and wood repairs. When she heard that a specialist in tree preservation had been called to inspect and make recommendations for the trees, she gave her a big smile. "The place would not be right without the trees."

Frances asked Mrs. Stubblefield if she would be able to meet with them one day and look at some of the items they wanted to use. She replied that she was now using a cane and had been trained on going up and downstairs. They set a date for the next week for the trip, during which they planned to have lunch at the house.

Chapter 22

On the designated Sunday, they had decided to make a party of Mrs. Stubblefield's visit to her home. The group that had been working at the warehouse brought their families and started by setting up tables on the side porch for lunch. Each table had crisp linens and fresh flowers. They had decided to use different patterns of china and crystal for the tables rather than matching. This way they could experiment with how each grouping looked.

Sam and Otis had been busy planting flowers in the yard, and the profusion of color gave a new life to the property. Margaret and Connie had given Mrs. Stubblefield's personal rooms a special cleaning, and when she walked in, she felt she had never been away. Frances felt the rooms knew their mistress was about to return and they wanted to please her.

While Frances stood in the sitting room and looked around, she wondered if Mrs. Stubblefield would be offended if she asked how long she had been living in the two rooms. Everything was still in the same spot when Frances first viewed the rooms, but there was definitely life here now.

Louise had taken charge of the food. She had coordinated the dishes that each person would bring. When Frances walked over to the tables where the food had been placed, she could smell the aroma that she remembered from her wedding day. "Welcome to Fatville!" she said as she peeked under the covered dishes.

Everyone could feel the excitement in the air around the house before they heard the car coming up the driveway. Frances stood still on the porch, trying to understand the change. It was almost as if the house, trees, flowers, and air had sensed her coming. Does the house know the sacrifice Mrs. Stubblefield made to keep it?

Everyone had gathered at the edge of the driveway to welcome Mrs. Stubblefield back to her home. It reminded Frances of stories of servants lining up to welcome new brides to old estates.

When Joseph opened the door for Mrs. Stubblefield to get out, she stood in place for a minute before speaking. She held her face up to the wind and sun and closed her eyes. The only sound that could be heard was wind rustling through the leaves of the trees. It made a sound that was almost like applause. Tears ran from beneath Mrs. Stubblefield's closed eyelids and a smile came across her face like that from an angel.

She opened her eyes, held out her arms. "God bless you, one and all!" It was almost a stampede of everyone wanting to embrace her at the same time. There were tears in everyone's eyes. Everyone walked around the yard, admiring the work that had been done. It was unbelievable the progress the plants had made in such a short time. The Morris brothers said they only needed to be reminded that someone still cared for them.

When they went up the steps to the front porch, the rockers had a fresh coat of paint and the pots of flowers were in full bloom. The shutters across the front had been repaired and freshly painted. The brass on the front door had been polished and the glass was sparkling clean.

Otis explained that they had not yet done anything to the foyer. There would be tracking, and it would be one of the last projects. The banister going up the stairs had been sanded and caulked. The dining room had been painted and the floors cleaned and polished. The doors of the built-in china cabinets were open and the inside was being made ready for china and crystal to be placed inside.

Cloths still remained on the floors of the living room. They could see where someone was working on the wiring for the chandelier. Repairs were being made to the fire brick and a new damper was on the floor in front of the fireplace.

As the group went out to the rear porch, they busied themselves on purpose to allow Mrs. Stubblefield to go to her private rooms alone. Frances had not said anything to anyone, but it was as if it was an unspoken understanding this should be a private time for her.

After about two minutes, Mrs. Stubblefield came back to the door. "Aren't you going to see what has happened in here? It is unbelievable. You cannot find anything that has been moved since I left, with the exception of the dust is gone."

While they were eating, Mrs. Stubblefield asked Frances how she planned to use the house. Frances, with the help of her friends, outlined how they wanted to have the antiques displayed in the house and have receptions, tours, weddings, and other functions. Mrs. Stubblefield asked her if she planned to take care of the house herself.

Frances said they currently did not have time and would have to find someone that would be qualified to take care of the house. In addition to maintaining the house, they would have to coordinate the social functions. She asked Mrs. Stubblefield if she knew anyone who might do that. Mrs. Stubblefield was silent for a few moments, then finally said she did not know anyone. She had been so isolated that she no longer knew people.

Frances said when the time was right, the person would come to them.

Joseph could tell Mrs. Stubblefield was getting tired and suggested that she go home to rest and come back again soon.

Everyone gave hugs of farewell and waved as the car drove back down the lane.

Frances stood alone, watching the car turn onto the main road. She was still standing there when she saw a car slow down as it passed in front of the property. Still feeling paranoid from the experience with the two intruders at the barn, she started walking down the driveway. As she got nearer the car, she could see a blond female in the front seat. She had a camera focused on the house and did not hear Frances approaching. When she saw her, she was startled at first and then regained her composure. The car door car opened, and she stood smiling at Frances.

The lady extended her hand. Frances took her hand and looked up. She was tall, trim, and very pretty. "I hope you do not mind that I was photographing your house. I should have asked. I had driven down the coast to Marshland to visit friends and was headed back to Atlanta when I saw the house. I could not resist taking a picture. It is so beautiful. I had never noticed it before, and I don't know how I could have missed such a pretty house."

Frances felt an immediate liking of the woman. She was open and honest. "Would you like to see more? It is a work in progress, but we are proud. Do you like old homes?"

The woman was almost prancing. "You would let me see inside? I would love it!"

Frances went around the front of the car and opened the passenger door. "We always drive around to the back. You can park and you can meet the others."

Everyone was still sitting on the porch at the tables when the car came around the driveway. Iced tea glasses stopped in midair, and everyone was looking to see who was coming. Frances got out of the car and announced, "We have our first official person to tour the house."

The lady was out of the car and up the steps before anyone could regain their thoughts. She was shaking hands and smiling at everyone and telling them she was Mrs. Waller.

Louise cleared the place where Mrs. Stubblefield had been sitting and offered to fix Mrs. Waller a plate. Mrs. Waller shook her head and then spied the pie. "Now the pie, I can't refuse."

Frances saw the expression on the woman's face as she saw the place settings on the tables. When she had been served, she took a bite, closed her eyes, and said, "This is unbelievable."

When they had finished, everyone started clearing the tables. Mrs. Waller started helping as if she had always been with the group.

Connie was at the sink washing dishes as they were brought to her and Gail was drying them and putting them back into the cartons. Mrs. Waller was looking at the two rooms and touched the afghan that was draped across Mrs. Stubblefield's chair. She walked over to the pictures on the wall and stood studying each one. Frances suddenly worried that she had made a mistake inviting a stranger into the house.

Mrs. Waller turned around when she sensed Frances in the room. "This is a special room. Who does it belong to?"

Frances explained about Mrs. Stubblefield and her circumstances. Mrs. Waller listened to Frances's explanation and what she planned to do with the house. "This is great. You are a special person to want to share what you have with others."

They had started walking toward the main part of the house while Frances was talking. Frances said, "I don't feel this belongs to me. I feel we have all been here to be caretakers for our past and to preserve the future. What good would it do me if I were to deny others of the beauty?"

As they walked around the rooms, Mrs. Waller bubbled with pleasure. The others had come into the rooms and the Morris boys were running around explaining what the plans were for the rooms. Mrs. Waller was telling them of some architectural details she had seen in some old houses and they were latching on to every word she was saying. They were like three children turned loose in a toy store.

Doris was leaning against a door frame, and when she got Frances's attention, she was nodding her head in a manner Frances could not interpret. Frances eased her way over to where she was standing and Doris pulled her into the next room. "What about her?"

Frances thought she was uneasy about allowing her know so much about their plans. "I wondered about that too, but I think she's safe. She seems to be a nice person, and I like her."

"No," Doris whispered, "that is not what I meant." By this time, all the other women had left the trio and had joined in the huddle. "She sounds like she knows about old houses and furnishings—maybe she would be interested in managing the house."

Frances shook her head. "She lives in Atlanta, and that is a long drive to get to work."

"Well, I thought it was a good idea," Nadine said. The others nodded in agreement.

Mrs. Waller's voice caught them off guard. "There you are!" They all sprang around as if they had been doing something wrong. Frances was sure Mrs. Waller had seen them whispering and was probably hurt by their rudeness. Anxious to make amends, Frances decided the best thing to do would be to tell the truth.

When Mrs. Waller heard what they were saying, she was surprised. "You're kidding! You would let me help with the house? I would love it. I have told my friends for years if I could find something to do in Marshland, I would be here in a flash."

Frances asked cautiously, "You would be interested?"

Mrs. Waller embraced Frances with a hug. "Interested! I'm ecstatic. I can as soon as I can get my personal belongings from Atlanta?"

All the women said at the same time, "The sooner, the better!"

Peggy extended her hand. "Welcome to Synaxis, Mrs. Waller."

Mrs. Waller returned the handshake and said, "I think you should call me by the name my friends use, Lecie."

Chapter 23

Frances was lounging in her bath that evening with the three cats in a circle around her. "I have really been ignoring you lately. What have you been doing for entertainment?"

Sunshine stood and peered over the side of the tub at her. Star was busy washing her face and Zeus was starring at her as if to say, "You are not going to get off that easy."

When Frances was dressing for bed, she opened a drawer and saw the brass key where she had placed it for safe keeping. Picking it up, she turned to Zeus. "Are you not going to tell me where you found this key?" She only received a stare that told her the answer was no.

Walking from the room, she started up the hall, pausing at each door. "I guess it is not material where you found the key, but what does the key fit?" Each time she would stop, the three cats at her heels would stop and sit. She examined the doors to the rooms and the key fit none of them. She ended up in the sanctuary where she sat down on her pew. Tapping the key in her hand, she looked around. It was not to the front door because that was a larger key. The door to the belfry did not have a lock. It did not fit the lock to the basement door. She went to the room that had been a storage room or office. The key did not fit the door. Inside the area were boxes, file cabinets, and an assortment of nondescript items.

Making sure none of the cats were inside, she closed the door. Leaning against the frame, she looked around. She saw the door to the basement, but thought everything had been moved to the warehouse. Still, she headed in that direction. She had never been downstairs at night, and she had never been downstairs alone. She opened the door at the top of the stairs and turned on the first light. She looked down at her feet and all three cats were standing beside her and looking down the steps. "You want me to go first and make sure it's safe?"

Each step she took, a cat would follow, never getting in front of her. When she got to the bottom of the stairs, they still remained at her side. The basement had been cleared of all the crates and someone had even swept the floor. Frances walked around in the room looking at the walls. The brick work was beautiful. She touched the wall and could tell it had been constructed from hand-formed brick. The mortar joints had been constructed by someone proud of their work. She was examining the floor that had probably been poured after the church was built. That was probably one of the reasons for the outside exit. One of the owners of the church had done this to expand the storage. Why did they continue to secure more storage rather than dispose of some of the antiques? Had they perhaps sold some of the pieces?

She and the cats were moving around the walls back toward the steps when Frances looked toward the steps. Suddenly, she noticed a door beneath the steps, in the shadows. When she reached the door, she got hold of the knob and slowly turned it. It was locked. One of the cats brushed her ankle as it went around her. She could feel her heart beating rapidly. She eased the key into the lock and gave it a turn. She heard an audible click as the tumblers made a connection. The sound made an echo in the empty basement. Sunshine gave a little jump. Frances had her hand ready to open the door when she heard Joseph's voice upstairs: "Where are you, Frances?"

The cats almost ran over each other going up the stairs. Frances went to the bottom of the steps and called out, "I'm down here." She could hear his footsteps as he came through the sanctuary. She could feel the relief in her body as he came down the steps. Leaning over to see her, he asked, "What are you doing down here at this time of night?"

"I came across the key that Zeus had left for me, and I was suddenly curious about what it would open. I have found the door it fits and was just starting to open it. I'm glad you're here because it is rather spooky down here at night."

Joseph came to her and put his arm around her for comfort. "Are you ready?"

Frances nodded.

The door opened with one of the loudest squeaks Frances had ever heard. They both laughed. "Did you bring a flashlight?" he asked.

"No, you know I never go prepared. Anyway, this was unexpected."

Joseph and Frances slowly eased into the opening. There was the usual string hanging down for a light just about a foot inside. When Joseph pulled the string, a bright light illuminated the area, which turned out to be a small office containing a wooden desk and chair with wooden file cabinets of the same era as at the warehouse. There were a few papers on top of the desk. On top of the desk was a lamp. Joseph switched it on and a soft light reflected on the surface of the desk.

Frances sat down in the chair and opened a drawer. Inside were bound ledgers. She opened the one on top and the date shown at the top of the page was 1949. In neat columns were descriptions of items and a monetary listing, with a brief description of the source of the item. The last entry was dated 1951. All the pages in the ledger were not completed. This was obviously when someone quit listing the items or stopped acquiring anything.

The next book down started at 1937 and ended in 1949. The next book started at 1929 and went to 1937. The oldest listing in the ledgers was 1759. There was no indication of who had made the entries, just listings.

Frances and Joseph put the books back in the drawer in the same order they had been removed. They opened the drawers on the other side of the desk and found it was full of journals. The top journal was dated 1951. Frances flipped the pages to find the last entry, made July 20, 1951.

The writing appeared to have been by the same person who had made the entry in the ledger for that period. The ink had faded but was still legible.

My sons are lazy. I cannot persuade one of them to visit Synaxis with me. They would prefer to live their fast lives with the money I have given them. I realize my mistakes now, but it is too late. I should have done as my father before me. My first visit to the antiques was at the age of six. I was taught this belongs to us. He never let me know what was expected of me, I just continued to collect as he had done. He told me on my first visit I should not talk about the antiques. If the family found out there would be nothing left. "Always guard the legacy." I have done as I was told.

I have guarded the antiques for sixty years. I moved them to Synaxis forty years ago. The location was perfect. Too many people were asking questions before. No one asked any questions here. It does not look as if anyone has ever been here.

I am tired; my illness leaves me no energy. I have sent a key to my friend Whitehead with instructions to dispose of the property in the event of my death, if one of my sons does not want the property.

When I walked through the rooms, tears came to my eyes. I remember the day everything was transferred here. So much has been added under my watch. What is the purpose of my collection? Has it brought inspiration or admiration from my fellow man?

No, I have only hoarded to keep others from having. The only pleasure in life has been obtaining what someone else owned. What is having without sharing?

I will go back to Savannah today and rest so I can return to finish the last pieces I brought.

The entry ended and there were no other entries after July 20, 1951. The person must have died or was unable to return. Why did Mr. Whitehead wait so long to sell the property?

Frances and Joseph placed the journal back in the drawer. Joseph turned out the light and locked the door as they left. Silently, they went up the stairs to find the three cats sitting at the top waiting for them.

When Frances and Joseph sat down in the kitchen, she said, "We will have to read more of the journals to find out where it all started."

Zeus reached his paw up to her and she reached down to pick him up. Holding him close, she could feel his purr. "You know you did well." Zeus raised his head and looked at her with large golden eyes.

Chapter 24

It was decided that they needed to have a meeting to regroup and plan. Things had been happening faster than anyone thought. The auction in Ashville had been a success, and the auction house had starting asking when they could receive another shipment. It was unanimous that no other items would be sacrificed.

Peggy told them how much money had been accumulated in the account and how much Sam and Otis thought renovations were going to cost for the mansion. Estimates for salaries and upkeep for the house were calculated. Finances still looked good.

Mrs. Williams said she had sent inquiries to several museums and had started receiving requests. They needed to decide which items they were going to use in the mansion and which items they could start circulating to the museums. Lecie would return from Atlanta in two days and that would help in selections. The pieces could be shipped to the museums in the crates that had been used at the church.

It was decided they needed to work in the attic at the mansion one day to organize the articles and see what could be used downstairs. Frances told them of the clothes and how beautiful they would be displayed in the bedrooms. They needed to find someone who knew how to clean the clothes. They made a note for the cleaning as well as mending of the clothes.

J. T. said he knew of a man who used to restore antiques. He had not seen him in a while, but would check to see if he were able to help them with the furniture in the attic.

The group decided to go out to the mansion to start working on the attic. Doris asked Frances if she would mind bringing the cats. "If we get their scent in the attic, it will discourage mice. You don't want to see me when I see a mouse—we would have major renovations on our hands."

They got out the traveling cases and called to the trio. They all came trotting and went to their respective carriers without a complaint.

When they arrived, Sam and Otis helped them move the cats into the house. When they were released, they started their re-inspection. They examined every room on the first floor before going up the stairs, then repeated their process, and finally made their way up the steps to the attic where the work had begun.

The work group was wandering around the area, trying to decide where to start. The lighting was poor in a lot of the areas. A lot of the articles had no significant historical value. One of the options was to have a sale to dispose of those items. Perhaps they could have it at the loading dock at the warehouse. Also, some of the items could be set up in the office. They could put flyers in some of the stores at Marshland to create interest.

After three hours of sorting and carrying loads down the stairs, the group stopped for a break. Star and Sunshine had followed everyone down to the kitchen and had curled up in a sunny spot to take a nap. When Frances realized Zeus had not followed them, she went back to the main house to call. She stood in the front hall calling to him and would listen for the sound of him coming down the stairs. She advanced to the second floor and repeated her calls. When she did not hear any response, she went up the stairs to the attic.

Frances stood at the entrance to the attic and listened for any movement. The only sound that could be heard was the sound of birds outside and the wind as it moved through the leaves. She repeated in a low voice, "Zeus, where are you?" She tried to remember if they could have closed him inside one of the boxes or trunks. She moved quietly around the room, listening for any sound. He would surely cry or scratch trying to get out.

She heard the sound of voices as the group returned up the stairs. When they reached the top of the stairs and saw her, they realized that something was not right. As soon as she explained to them her fears, everyone started opening all the trunks and cases, searching for the missing cat. The light in the attic was beginning to get dim. The sun had moved and was no longer helping. Sam and Otis had walked around outside trying to see if he could have gotten out by accident.

Everyone was secretly glancing at each other, not wanting to upset Frances. When they were satisfied that every container had been searched, they gathered at the top of the stairs. Nadine tried to talk to Frances in a calm voice. "I know you don't want to leave without him, but we have searched inside everything. Sam and Otis have checked all the screens, and there is no way he could have gotten outside. We'll come back first thing in the morning and start looking again."

Frances tried to keep the tears from pouring over her eyelids. She had never left the cats alone before. The thought of Zeus being in the house alone and afraid broke her heart. There was no way she could stay. Sam told her they had already put Star and Sunshine in their carriers. Everyone started down the stairs. Frances looked back around the room one last time before she left.

Someone stopped to check the front door to make sure it was locked. When the group got to the back hall, Otis, who was leading the line, stopped suddenly. "Well, I'll be!" Perched on top of his carrier sat the black cat, in the process of washing behind one of his ears. As they all stood staring at him, he looked at them with one paw in midair and gave them the golden eye stare. "What?"

"Where have you been?" Frances said, in a voice loud and fierce. The cat, realizing he had done something wrong, jumped down from the top of the carrier and immediately ran inside for protection.

Chapter 25

To say that Lecie Waller came to town like a whirlwind would be an apt description. Frances silently compared the way she herself had come to town a few months ago to Lecie's arrival. Lecie was pulling a small moving trailer behind her car, which was loaded almost to the point of her not being able to get in to drive.

She pulled beside the warehouse, and someone sounded the alarm for everyone to go outside and see the site. As the group lined up on the platform looking down at the car, Lecie bounced out and spread her arms wide. "When I come to stay, I come to stay!"

Nadine went down the steps to greet her. "How did you find us?"

"Well, I was going through town to the mansion and was looking at all the buildings when I spotted all of your cars. If you want to hide, you'll have to come up with a better plan."

Peggy walked around the car and trailer once, and then said, "Why don't we put everything in the small office in the back until she's ready to get her belongings in order?"

Lecie opened the trunk and the doors of the trailer and the procession resembled a line of ants carrying bounty to the hill.

Margaret examined the boxes. "I never saw anyone so organized. Every box is labeled with exactly what's in it and where the items should be placed when unpacked. Girl, do you want to come to my house and help me?"

Frances piped up, "I'm next!"

Gail leaned over to Lecie. "You better take a look at Frances's home before you make any promises. It takes a lot of boxes."

Frances displayed an exaggerated expression of hurt. "You can walk down the hall, I have several empty rooms and my basement is spotless. I'm still a work in progress."

From the short time she had watched them, Lecie knew there had to be a big story behind the story.

Peggy glanced at her watch. "Let's call the guys and have them pick up dinner and initiate Lecie properly. We can drop off some of the cars and not have so many to drive home."

Lecie followed Doris to her home and they left their cars and got in with Frances. As they passed the service station, Frances rolled down her window, Doris rolled down her window in the back. Frances honked the horn and they both waved. Lecie looked puzzled. "What is that all about?"

Frances looked in her rearview mirror at Doris. "We're just ordering tea. If one person waves, we only need one jug. If two people wave, we need two."

Lecie sat quietly for a few minutes and finally asked, "Don't we need to stop to get it?"

Doris in her long drawl replied, "No, they deliver."

Chapter 26

When the car turned down the lane leading to the church, Frances glanced in the rearview mirror at Doris who winked. She slowed the car for the full effect of the arrival. Lecie was looking at the water and cypress and as they neared the church, her face lit up. "What a beautiful setting for a church. You'd never believe it would be in this remote location." As they started through the cemetery, she tried to ask politely, "Is this a shortcut to your home?"

Frances and Doris had to work hard not to laugh. As they came out of the cemetery and neared the back of the church, Lecie exclaimed, "I don't think I ever remember seeing a church with a screened porch and a three-car garage."

Frances parked the car and looked over at Lecie, who had the most bewildered expression. "You live in a church?"

All three cats were waiting at the door for Frances. When Lecie saw them, she forgot all about Frances living in a church or anyone else being around. She literally sat down in front of them and was taking turns holding and inspecting each in turn. They were eating up the attention from someone new. When one was not being held, it was walking around Lecie and rubbing its head against her.

When the rest of the group arrived, Lecie stood and announced, "I think I'm ready to see your home." They started through the rooms with everyone explaining what all had been done and how much had been there from the beginning.

Cars started arriving and food was being brought in. Tables, chairs, and plates were organized, as someone counted heads to make sure there were enough chairs for everyone. Lecie was startled when she heard the siren. "What's happening?"

Someone said, "Don't worry, that's just the tea arriving."

Lecie almost immediately fit right into the group, and once in the circle, it was as if she had always been with them.

After dinner, they discussed the best way to start work in the morning. They decided to start removing the items in the attic and take them down to the warehouse, then start getting ready for the yard (or platform) sale. The afternoon could be used to start cleaning the house, from the top down.

After everyone had left, Frances and Joseph propped up in bed to read more of the journal Joseph had brought upstairs.

> *I do not know if I should have told Whitehead more about the church. I only told him it was an old building that had not been used in years. I explained to him I used the property to store excess materials I purchased and did not have space in Savannah to accommodate the boxes. I mentioned that my family did not have an interest in the property.*
>
> *It is becoming more difficult to locate quality pieces. Families are becoming more aware of the value of their heritage. Others that did not know the value destroyed pieces that cannot be replaced. I am concerned about the future of the collection. Will someone else share my love for the past?*
>
> *I realize I should have taken someone into my confidence when I first realized my wife was going to make our children dependent their entire lives. You cannot give people the desire*

> *to achieve—it must be gained by doing. When I am gone, they will become destitute.*
>
> *I look back through the journals and I do not know where everything is stored. I know it is on this property, but have lost control of the records. The burden has become overwhelming. Never in the years did I believe the line would end with me.*

Frances and Joseph stopped reading. They were both silent for several minutes. Frances spoke almost in a whisper, "I'm so glad I'm the person who was given the opportunity to care for these antiques. I can only imagine what would have happened if they'd been trusted to some unscrupulous person who only cared about the money."

Joseph did not respond immediately. After a while, his tone was as serious. "One thing certain, he was fortunate to have found this location. Other than the problem brought on by the people in Atlanta, this location is safe. The people of Synaxis are honest and caring. I'm sure they will continue to help you. Rarely do you find a group of people willing to help each other without expectation of reward."

As they turned out the lights, all three cats stood up, stretched, and repositioned themselves for the night. There was the sound of a soft purr for a few minutes and then all was silent.

Chapter 27

Bright and early the next morning, everyone met at the warehouse. Frances and the others could not believe all they had accomplished. Sam and Otis said all the repairs had been made, the house had been cleaned, and all was ready for the selections to be taken to the mansion.

Connie, Margaret, and Louise had taken care of the draperies, which were folded over hangers that had been placed on rolling racks. They thought this would be the easiest way to transport. It was decided that the draperies should be their first task. Everyone gathered their tools, the racks were pushed on the enclosed van, and the caravan made its way to the mansion.

It seemed as if they hung draperies every day. By lunchtime, all the windows were covered, and everyone had walked from room to room, admiring their work. Peggy had disappeared and called from the porch. "Lunch is ready." Everyone rushed out to see the baskets she had placed at the tables.

"When did you have time for all this?"

"The chicken had been cooked and put in the freezer. You just thaw, throw in a food processor, line up the bread, smear, and stack. It's easy."

"It's easy if you're not dragging three cats who are hanging on to your ankles waiting for you to drop something," Frances remarked.

In the afternoon, they walked from room to room, deciding what pieces to bring first. Each person was making a list for the room they were going to assemble. They were about ready to go to the warehouse and load the truck for the first load when they heard a car coming up the driveway. Sam looked out the window and announced that it was Joseph, with two ladies.

As they were coming down the stairs, Joseph opened the door and led the two ladies into the foyer. The strangers were not at first aware of anyone else as they looked from room to room.

Frances went over to Joseph and he gave her a quick embrace, then with his arm still around her waist, he started making introductions. The older lady was Grace and the younger was her daughter, Anne. Joseph explained that Anne was getting married in three months and the place that was going to have the reception was not going to be able to fulfill the contract. They were trying to find other arrangements when one of Joseph's associates told them to talk to him. He brought them out to see the mansion and see if anything could be done.

Frances looked at the others and told Grace and her daughter that they had not planned on getting ready that soon. As everyone in the group saw the disappointed look on Anne's face, they each felt guilty. Lecie, who was still standing halfway up the stairs, took a few steps down. "Well, it will take a lot of work, but I think we can do it." When everyone else agreed, they sat down with the bride and started a new list: How did she want her reception?

When they had finished all the arrangements and were preparing to leave, Anne and her mother hugged everyone, telling them how grateful they were for their help. Anne's parting words were that it was going to be the best reception ever!

As they stood waving at the departing car, they heard the truck start behind them. When they came up beside them, Otis asked, "Are you going to stand there or are we going to get moving?"

Everyone yelled together, "We're moving!"

The next day, Mrs. Williams, Lecie, and Peggy went to the mansion ahead of the truck to help with setup. Nadine had the computer printing out lists for the others to assemble near the dock to be loaded on the truck. Gail and Margaret were packing the china and crystal in boxes to be transported.

By late afternoon, everyone had gathered to assemble the rooms. The parlor was complete, and they stood at the door looking at their hard work. Connie said, "It looks as if it's always been this way."

Each day during the remainder of the week was a repeat of the first day. No one complained of being tired; the excitement of their task gave them energy. Frances decided she was just getting accustomed to working.

The ladies were standing in one of the bedrooms when they heard the men coming up the stairs. From the sounds, they knew they were carrying something, but could not figure out what. When Don backed into the room, he was carrying a large covered piece.

Kevin and Jason were trying to squeeze through the door with the bundle. J. T. was giving directions and they finally got through the door. Placing the large object in a corner, J. T. turned and asked, "Are y'all ready?" The ladies all nodded.

When the cover was removed, they saw a beautiful display case holding the heirloom wedding dress. The room was so silent. Someone sniffed and said, "Oh my."

"When we saw all the lace in this room, we decided this was where it belonged." Again, all was silent.

They locked the doors and made their way to the vehicles. Frances looked at some of the houses on the way home. She could swear she could see fresh paint and flowers that she had not noticed before. *It couldn't be*, she thought. An entire town doesn't decide to change.

She saw Joseph behind her and they gave each other a little wave. When they pulled in the driveway, Star and Zeus were sitting at the screen and Sunshine came through the cat door with a long stretch and a yawn.

Chapter 28

As they were working with Anne on the arrangements for the reception, they asked if they could invite Mrs. Stubblefield. They explained about her life at the mansion and what they felt it would mean to her to be included. Both Anne and Grace absolutely wanted her to be included; they felt it would give added meaning to the event.

Frances and Peggy went to the retirement home and took the old lady shopping. After she had selected the outfit she wanted, they found a beauty shop and made arrangements for her to have a special hairstyle the morning of the reception. The retirement home would provide transportation to the hairdresser, and then Joseph would bring her to the mansion.

The group spent hours outlining the food, decorations, and individual responsibilities for the event. Later, they would establish procedures and train local people to help. Lecie had already started books and had outlines on the computer.

The morning of the reception, they gathered in the kitchen at the mansion. Ron was able to get appliances, Sam and Otis had built storage cabinets and work tables with shelves beneath for easy food preparation. Everyone had decided to dress in navy skirts and white shirts. They put their assembly line in operation, and soon, the double refrigerator with glass doors displayed an array of trays garnished ready for the guests to arrive.

It was agreed that Joseph would bring Mrs. Stubblefield two hours before the reception was scheduled so she could see the house. When she walked in the door, the pleasure on her face was all they needed to know they had done a good job. Sam and Otis escorted her around the rooms and she admired every detail.

When the line made the ascent to the second floor, they could not wait for Mrs. Stubblefield's comments. They ended up in what they had all called *The Bride's Room*. When she smiled and said, "It's my dress!" all twelve women were dabbing their eyes. Frances heard Joseph tiptoe away, and in a few minutes, she heard the noise of him blowing his nose. Mrs. Williams went over to her and put her arm around her.

Mrs. Stubblefield said, "This was my room when I dressed for my wedding. I was so happy. My grandmother said I was the prettiest bride yet to wear the dress. I was the last to wear the dress."

When we went back downstairs, Mrs. Stubblefield said she would like to sit in one of the freshly painted rockers on the front porch and enjoy the yard. Otis and Sam came back to the kitchen and said they thought she would just like to be alone for a while.

After the guests were gone and the rooms restored, everyone sat down to rest and compare notes. One thing was unanimous: everyone thought the place was wonderful. Lecie said she already had three bookings just from the guests today. Mrs. Stubblefield said she had not been happier in years, seeing everyone enjoying the house.

She had stayed in the rocking chair throughout most of the afternoon. Every guest, including the men, came by and thanked her for letting the property be used for the enjoyment of others. Many had admired the home all their lives and wondered who lived there.

Sam and Otis said they had never enjoyed a project as much as the restoration of this house. People say it is a full-time job taking care of a place like this. Sam and Otis hoped they were right.

After Joseph drove home and they settled down with their cats, he looked over at Frances. "Could you even imagine two years ago that you would be doing something like this?"

Frances closed her eyes and a tear ran down her cheek. "I didn't know a person could feel so good about something. The day I arrived here and thought I had lost everything was a lesson for me. If you look at what you're given in life and think you have nothing, then that is what you get. But if you look at what has been given to you and share it with others, you will be rewarded. My new home gave you back to me, gave me a town full of friends, and the opportunity to let millions of people enjoy the beauty of the past. I am the richest woman in the world."

Zeus jumped up in her lap, carrying the small journal he had found in the attic. Frances took it from him. "Thank you." Star and Sunshine climbed up beside them. Frances opened the journal to the first page and looked at the neat writing. "You three are going to have to wait until later for me to read to you. First, we're going to rest."

About the Author

Ellen Tucker lives in north Georgia with her husband and three cats—Star, Zeus, and Sunshine. Many of the adventures in the book are inspired by the actions of their lives together.